TRILLIONS

Also by the same author:

Flip Side
Mind Benders

TRILLIONS

Nicholas Fisk

Hodder
Children's
Books

a division of Hodder Headline plc

Copyright © 1971 Nicholas Fisk

First published in Great Britain in 1971
by Hamish Hamilton

Second edition published in Great Britain in 1977
by Penguin Books Ltd.

This edition published in Great Britain in 1998
by Hodder Children's Books

The right of Nicholas Fisk to be identified as the Author of the
Work has been asserted by him in accordance with
the Copyright, Designs and Patents Act 1988.

10 9 8 7 6 5 4 3 2 1

A Catalogue record for this book is
available from the British Library

ISBN 0340 71021 7

Typeset by
Palimpsest Book Production Limited

Printed and bound in Great Britain by
Clays Ltd, St Ives plc

Hodder Children's Books
A Division of Hodder Headline plc
338 Euston Road
London NW1 3BH

Written for Nim

Chapter One

No one can tell you exactly who it was now, but it was quite certainly one of the youngest children that invented the name 'Trillions' You can imagine a group of children squatting on the ground, scraping together heaps of brightly coloured, mysterious grit that had fallen from the sky . . .

'I've got millions!'

'I've got billions!'

'I've got *trillions!*'

Trillions it was from then on. The name fitted perfectly. It had the right hard, bright sound to it – and Trillions were hard and bright. It suggests millions upon millions – and the Trillions were everywhere, sprinkling roads and gardens and roofs and even the firesides of people's homes with a glittery dusting of tiny jewels (but Trillions were not jewels).

And the name Trillions had a foreign sound to it – a suggestion of other worlds, star-studded skies, the cold emptiness of space. That was right, too. For wherever Trillions came from, it was not this world.

So everyone – the children, then the adults, then the local newspapers, then the national newspapers and TV stations and at last the world authorities – came to call the strange, jewel-like dust by the name the children invented: Trillions.

It is strange about names. Ten years before the Trillions came, Mr and Mrs Harding had christened their well behaved, sandy-haired baby 'James'. When he was five, it was found that he would have to wear spectacles, so James Harding became Specs. When he was six or seven, his schoolfriends began to call him Prof, because his appearance reminded them of an absent-minded professor.

But this name was wrong too: James turned out to be anything but absent-minded. In fact, he was the very opposite. He was the sort of boy who wanted a place for everything and everything in its place. He wanted hard facts, not soft opinions. When he had got the facts right, he would act.

It was James who solemnly, earnestly and thoroughly cleared the name of the oil-delivery man who was accused – wrongly – of stealing central-heating oil from the tanker he drove, then selling it. (The local newspaper called James *The Boy Detective*, which made him furious. 'I am not a boy detective,' he said, 'I am someone who can do arithmetic.')

By then, James' name had already become Bem. Bem

suited him perfectly. It had the solid, sober feeling. And it sounded close to 'Ben'. In addition, it meant B.E.M. or Bug-Eyed Monster. For James, with his round face, round spectacles and passion for science, 'Bem' was the name that made sense.

Or – still talking about names – take Panda. Bem's eight-year-old sister was christened Penelope, rather a grand name. But even as a baby, she had been tiny, burning-eyed, round-faced yet spiky. Very soon her 'real' name suggested itself. Her eyes were black, and slightly shadowed; her skin was white; her face was round. What other name was there for her but Panda?

Mina, the Olivellis' girl who lived next door, needed no nickname. Mina – you say it 'Meena' – suited her perfectly. She was nine and a half, olive-skinned, black-haired, very slightly plump – Italian-looking. You could call her a female girl. If you dressed Mina in a top hat, lumberjack coat, riding breeches and coalminer's boots and finished off with a burnt-cork moustache, everyone would still say 'What a pretty girl!'

You can imagine for yourself how Mina responded to the Trillions. When they arrived, her large, dark-brown eyes widened and glistened. Her neat, long-nailed, tapered fingers began to prod and pick. By the end of that day, she had found out how to use Trillions. She used them to decorate herself.

Which leaves Scott Houghton.

Scott is the most important person in this story after the Trillions themselves, yet it is hard to find the right things to say about him. He was of average height for his age –

thirteen. His hair was average brown. So were his eyes. His school record was average or above average. He was averagely popular. He never had a nickname – you can hardly count 'Scotty' – because he was too average to need one.

He was also extraordinary. The things that made him so unusual were unknown to his friends and barely noticed by his parents, who took him for granted (which suited Scott very well). His extraordinary qualities are hard to explian. Is it extraordinary for a schoolboy to keep bees? Scott did and had done so for four years. To Mr Bygrave, the strange old man who had first interested him in bees, Scott was extraordinary because he came to know more than his teacher. At first, the man had said, 'Ah, you've got an instinct for them! That's what it is, an instinct!' Later, he changed his mind. It wasn't instinct that Scott had: it was ability to observe, study, think, compare, invent.

Most modern beekeepers nowadays use a gadget called the Bygrave Controlled Demand Winter Feeder. Only one beekeeper, Mr Bygrave, knows that it should have been called the 'Houghton' Feeder. For the invention was Scott's, made when he was eleven.

His other interests were just as extraordinary. Scott was given a toy star telescope – made a real one from a kit of parts – rapidly became an expert observer – quickly tired of observing – and spent hours, from then on, in comparing astronomy and astrology; he was trying to make sense of the battle between science and mysticism.

When there was a craze for guitars and folk singing at his school, Scott tried to find a form of guitar amplification that did not spoil the sound of the guitar. He failed, but found instead a method for making very small loudspeaker enclosures that could still deliver a good bass tone. The little transistor radio Scott had in his bedroom sounded like a big set with a twelve-inch speaker. His mother complained about the booming of the bass, so he turned a switch and cut it down. Now the set sounded like any other portable radio. It never occurred to Scott's mother to ask him how such a small radio could produce such big tone – mothers are not curious about such things. Nor did it ever occur to Scott to do anything about his loudspeaker invention – he had lost interest in the thing when he had got it working properly and had become interested instead in four-wheel drive for motor-cars. His room became a maze of Meccano and the little radio's batteries ran flat.

Scott never spoke about his ideas and inventions, not even to his father. He was, after all, a schoolboy. Why should his father, a grown man, be interested in schoolboy ideas? In fact, his interests were shared by only one other person – Bem. But Bem was younger than Scott and also perhaps a smaller-minded person. Bem had an 'old' mind, Scott had an ageless mind. So Scott was really alone with his extraordinariness.

Meanwhile, the ordinary world went on. Scott suffered cut knees, punches in the nose, sarcasm from the English teacher and falls off bicycles, just like everyone else; he enjoyed chocolate ice-cream, certain funny programmes on TV, air rifles and all the things that thousands and millions of other boys liked. He did not think himself extraordinary. He knew only that certain things that interested him might bore other people. So he kept his mouth shut. It seemed the simplest thing to do.

But when the Trillions came, everything about him and around him became complicated. For the Trillions were very extraordinary indeed and it was to take more than ordinary ways of thinking and acting to deal with them.

Much more.

Chapter Two

Just what were the Trillions?

Start at the beginning. Scott, Mina, Panda and Bem all lived in the same road in Harbourtown West. Once, this town had been a fishing village. Now, it was just a pleasant place to live, with pleasure boats of all shapes, sizes and colours filling the harbour. Scott's father ran the yachting marina and made a comfortable living from it.

The important thing about Harbourtown West, as far as the Trillions were concerned, was that the place was situated on a narrow spur of land sticking out into the ocean. Harbourtown could be a windy, stormy place to live. It could get weather that no one else got.

On a sunny but windy day in May, Harbourtown and Harbourtown alone received a heavy shower of Trillions.

There was no rain and no cloud. In the windy, open sky there was a slight darkening – a cloudy patch that glittered in the sunlight. Then there was the sandstormy, rattling hiss as the Trillions came. Their showering lasted perhaps fifteen minutes. When it was over, there were drifts of Trillions everywhere. Trillions packed inches deep against a garden fence; Trillions glittering in drifts over roads and gardens; Trillions caught between the windows and window frames of houses and cars; Trillions edging the gutters, sparkling in the clefts of branches, lying thinly on the roofs of cars.

A few people were frightened by the Trillions. Most were puzzled and curious. The children were excited. 'I've got millions . . . billions . . . Trillions!' they cried.

While the other children squeaked and jumped or sifted and sorted the Trillions, Bem collected a single jar full of them and walked down the road to Scott's house – and nearly collided with Scott, who was just leaving his house to visit Bem.

'Come inside, Bem,' said Scott. 'What do you make of it?'

Bem did not answer for some time, then he said, 'Can we have a sheet of your father's layout paper from the big pad?'

'Sure. Hold on.'

Bem looked closely at his handful of Trillions.

'Make it four sheets.'

Scott came back with four large sheets of the half-transparent white paper and spread them on the floor.

'What are you going to do – sort them into sizes, or colours, or what?' he asked Bem.

'Sizes first. We could use strainers—'

'Yes, a wire coffee strainer and a nylon strainer. Two different sizes of mesh to begin with.'

Scott got the strainers from the kitchen. Bem took one strainer, then the other, and poured Trillions through them to grade them into two sizes. While he did this, he and Scott said nothing. They were used to doing things together.

They lay on the floor and studied the two heaps. A shaft of sunlight lit them and they glittered fiercely.

'They're beautiful,' said Scott, softly.

'Bigs and smalls. Most of the pale colours are smalls: most of the darker colours are bigs,' said Bem, without bothering to reply to Scott.

'Look at this sapphire one—'

'We need the microscope.'

'I'll get it,' said Scott, raising one eyebrow at Bem and smiling slightly.

'Yes, get it,' said Bem simply. Scott laughed to himself and went to get the microscope. It was always like this. Though Scott was older than Bem, it was Scott who fetched and carried. Not because Bem was selfish or rude, but because it never occurred to him to concentrate on more than one thing at a time. At this moment, he was concentrating on Trillions.

'Let's have it,' said Bem when Scott came back. Again Scott smiled. The microscope was his, Scott's.

'Here you are, you bossy little squirt,' said Scott.

For the first time, Bem looked up at him, startled. 'What did I—?'

'Never mind,' said Scott. 'Get on with it.'

Bem put a few Trillions on a dished glass slide, set up the microscope rapidly and peered into it.

'Two!' he said. 'That's odd. You look.'

'Two what?'

'Two sorts. See for yourself.'

Scott put his eye to the microscope. What he saw amazed and dazzled him. 'They're beaut—' he said, then remembered he had said it before. But they were beautiful all the same. It was as if he looked at priceless jewels, cut and facetted into superb circular gem-stones. Under the microscope, the colours were even more startling than they were under normal light. He increased the magnification to concentrate on one particular Trillion. It looked like a great ruby. Then he shifted the slide to what appeared as a giant emerald, with a thousand geometrical faces cut in it.

'Do you notice? Two sorts?' said Bem.

Scott looked again, comparing one Trillion with another.

'You're right, Bem. Two sorts Only two . . . One like a doughnut, with a hollow in the centre—'

'Not a hollow, a complete hole,' interrupted Bem.

'And the other with—'

'The other like a doughnut again, but with a spike sticking out of the centre. I suppose it's the same on both sides?'

Bem silently handed him a needle. Scott licked the point of it to make it sticky, touched the point to the Trillion and turned it over on the glass slide.

'Yes, the same both sides. Just the same. Like a jewelled doughnut with jewelled pyramids coming out of the centre. You could spin it like a top.'

'While the other sort has a hole in the centre . . . do you notice something else?'

'What about?'

'About the edges. Look at the way the outside edges are cut.'

Scott peered down the microscope, then lifted his head. His eye was watering.

'You should keep both eyes open, I've often told you—' said Bem.

'Oh, shut up. What do you mean about the edges? All I can see is a whole lot of regular triangular cuttings, like teeth in a gear wheel. The cuttings cover the whole of the outside of the doughnut shape—'

'Let me look for a moment,' said Bem, butting his head against Scott so that Scott had to move. Bem fiddled with the needle as he looked, then said 'Keep still. Don't jog me. Nearly there!'

He licked the needle again, and picked at the Trillions on the glass slide for a long time. Then said, 'Whatever you do, don't jog. But have a look!'

Scott carefully put his eye to the microscope. Bem, he saw, had moved two Trillions together so that they touched. Although the Trillions were of different sizes, they 'geared' together perfectly.

'They're like interlocking bricks – you know, those children's construction things!' said Scott. 'If you put a whole lot of Trillions they'd lock together!'

'That's not all. They fit together edge to edge, but they also fit together on top of each other. You can see how the ones with pyramids in the middle could

11

lock into the ones with doughnut holes. You could *build* with them!'

Scott sat back and stared at Bem. Bem stared owlishly back at him.

'What does it mean?' said Scott at last.

'I don't know.'

'Well, have you ever seen anything like it before? In nature, I mean?'

'I suppose there must be lots of things like it,' said Bem. 'But I just can't think of them. I mean, there's honeycomb, and crystals, and molecular structures – they all have shapes that fit together. But I can't think of anything just like this . . .'

Scott was about to look through the microscope again, when Bem's sister Panda came rushing in, trampling over the sheets of paper on the floor and shaking the microscope.

'Mind out!' shouted Bem, too late.

'They're *fantastic*!' shouted Panda. 'Oh, never mind the microscope, who cares about – they're *marvellous*!' She went on, 'I bet you don't know about them!'

'Know *what* about *what*?'

'About the Trillion things! They can do tricks! All on their own! Come and see!'

Chapter Three

It turned out that Panda – along with most of the children in Harbourtown West – had already discovered the most important and startling thing about Trillions. Just as she said, they could do tricks. All on their own.

'Watch!' she told Bem and Scott.

She squatted down on the stones of the patio, holding a piece of chalk. With this she made a simple squiggle – a rough 'S'. She scattered Trillions loosely over the 'S': then she sat back on her heels, looking triumphant.

'Well, what happens now?' demanded Bem.

'Wait!' said Panda. Everyone waited, silently.

It took about three minutes to happen.

Very slowly, piece by piece, the Trillions began to move. Looking closely, you could see one Trillion nudge another – gear with it – turn it – move it!

Then more Trillions would combine to form a geared-together mass. The process would go faster now. Some Trillions would lock with more Trillions, and still more, until the whole collection would shift and tumble like sand.

Scott looked quickly at Bem. His eyes and mouth were wide open.

At last, the Trillions finished their work. And now, replacing the 'S' that Panda had made, was another 'S' made entirely of Trillions. An 'S' correct in every detail, however tiny: where Panda's finger had slipped slightly and made a jerky curve, the Trillions' curve was jerky too. Where the chalk line was grainy, the Trillions' line was grainy.

The youngest children were shouting and laughing and pushing as they imitated Panda and made shapes of their own for the Trillions to imitate. Bem and Scott did not hear them. They stood in their own silence, staring and wondering. They walked back together, in silence, to Scott's house.

'Dad will be back about six,' said Bem at last. 'Perhaps he'll know something.'

Scott shook his head. 'He won't, nobody will. There's never been anything like this before. There just can't have been . . .'

There was silence for another minute or so. And then the cars started arriving.

'Your flash lead is pulled out,' Bem told the photographer.

'Thanks, son. Move over to one side a bit, would you? Thanks.'

Bem shrugged and walked on. There were cars everywhere, journalists and photographers everywhere, TV men everywhere. And everyone was in a hurry. The light was fading, the photographers were beginning to use flash to get their pictures.

'And what's your name, dear?'

Bem turned a cold eye on the TV woman and said, 'Bem, what's yours?' She turned away hurriedly and trapped Mina.

'And what's your name, dear?'

'Mina Olivelli, and I'm nine and a half in one month's time.'

A camera lurched overhead on its gantry, with a tough looking young man in control, and swooped on to Mina. 'And how do you feel about what's been happening here today in Harbourtown, Mina?'

'I'm collecting all the prettiest ones to make a bracelet!'

The camera came in still closer. Mina fluttered her eyelids at it, put her head on one side and beamed.

'And tell me, Mimi—'

'Mina. Mina Olivelli.'

'Tell me, Mina, how do you think the Trillions will change things in this little town?'

'Well, *my Daddy says* it's fan-tas-tic and my *Mummy* says oh dear what a mess to clear up, but *I say*—'

Bem groaned aloud and the TV woman looked furious. A sound engineer shouted, 'We picked up that groan, better forget it!'

Bem cheered up and walked on. *Bracelets* . . . !

A few hundred yards away, Scott and Panda were among

a group centred on a TV commentator, who was talking in preacher-like tones into his microphone, 'From the clear sky above us fell today a strange dust – a dust that could be a threat or a promise, a mysterious messenger from outer space or just the accidental sweepings of the universe . . .'

'Waffle,' said Scott.

The TV man extended the microphone to a white-haired but quite young-looking man in a trench coat, who seemed embarrassed.

'Well, we can't possibly give an explanation for a phenomenon that no one has had time to evaluate or examine . . .' he said, miserably.

'But tell me, Professor – with your unrivalled knowledge of conditions in outer space—'

'I haven't any unrivalled knowledge of outer space. No one has. I prefer not to be called "Professor".'

'What should I call you, sir? Flight Commander? – your rank when you—'

'—Never mind, forget it. I don't want to talk.'

The Professor or Flight Commander or whatever he was looked pitifully embarrassed now. He moved jerkily away and in doing so bumped into Panda.

He said, 'Oh, I am sorry.'

For some reason Scott wanted to talk to this odd-looking man, who seemed one of the few 'real' people there. He found courage to say to him,

'Excuse me, but I've looked at the Trillions under my microscope and they're very strange. I wish you could let me show you. Oh, I'm called Scott—'

'My name is Blythe—'

'This is Panda. Why don't you come and look for yourself?'

A few minutes later, there were more introductions when Blythe met Scott's parents and still more when Bem called in.

The man Blythe settled down with the microscope and for the first time, Scott had the chance to study him closely. What he saw puzzled him. He somehow knew the face but could not place it. Professor, Flight Commander or Mister Blythe was a strange mixture of youth and age. His eyes were remarkable: pale but dark-lashed, and brilliant. His hands were firm, hard and young – yet he used them nervously, sometimes clumsily. One hand moved woodenly as if it did not belong to the arm. The skin on his face and hands was strangely untidy in texture and colour – patchy – but smooth and unlined, except for a deep crease, a seam, on either side of his mouth. And this seam deepened whenever his mouth twitched, which was quite often. It was almost as if the professor was constantly biting back an unpleasant remark. Scott remembered a schoolmaster who had the same tight, nervous mouth, apparently bursting to say something that would never be said. But the schoolmaster had been a much older man.

Scott noticed another thing. Twice, Blythe put his right eye to the microscope, muttered something, peevishly – then used his left eye instead. Scott's father must have noticed too, for he asked. 'Can you handle the focusing all right? The coarse adjustment is on the lower wheel—'

Blythe replied, almost rudely, 'I know, I know!' Then, as if realizing he had sounded rude, said to Scott, This is a nice little instrument. Do you happen to have any polarizing screens? No? Well, never mind.'

After a long time, he took his eye from the microscope and sat upright, frowning.

Scott said, 'Well?'

Blythe looked blankly back at Scott and said, 'I could send you some polarizing screens, if you would like me to.'

'To make pretty coloured pictures? Thanks,' said Scott, coldly.

Blythe stared at him, then chuckled.

'Sorry,' he said.

'What do you think of them? The Trillions?' Scott insisted.

'Very interesting. Most unusual.'

Now he looked furtive – even shifty. Yet Scott still liked him, if 'like' is the word. There was a feeling of power about Blythe.

'The two shapes – and the toothed edges so that they can lock with each other –' said Scott, 'surely you noticed that?'

Blythe stood up, then sat down again. He rubbed his forehead and said, 'How old are you?'

'Thirteen. But I don't see—'

'And your friend – Ben, isn't it?'

'Bem. For Bug-eyed Monster. He's two years younger.'

'Well, your friend Panda's gone,' said Blythe, as if this was a good thing. 'So there's only us and you look sensible enough. And in any case, the papers, television – they'll all be full of it tomorrow. So what I think or say can't matter much . . .'

'What *do* you think?' said Scott's father, leaning forward.

'It's the fact that they form . . . make shapes . . . that's so extraordinary,' said Blythe. 'Extraordinary and frightening. Yes, I'm sorry, but I mean frightening. There's no parallel that I can think of, none at all. Sponges, great boulders said to move by themselves in the desert (did you hear about that? Fascinating) – coral reefs, molecules . . . There's nothing uncommon in things *forming* – in their developing shapes and structures.'

'But the Trillions *imitate*!'

'Yes, I was coming to that. As I was saying, there's nothing uncommon in things forming and growing – nature is full of elaborate structures. All quite usual. But then there's this question of mimicry. Almost instant mimicry. The Trillions can mimic and imitate. So can parrots. So can death-head moths. But they have taken countless years to learn their simple little tricks! While the Trillions—'

'Chameleons,' said Bem, suddenly.

'Quite right, chameleons. But it would be useless to expect a chameleon, for instance – and they are very advanced mimics, very good at it – to disguise themselves as a letter "S". Chameleons haven't many tricks. They don't have many ways of adapting themselves, camouflaging themselves. They just change colour. And chameleons – several fish and insects, too, for that matter – always alter their colour or pattern or shape for a limited purpose. Generally defence. But Trillions are doing exactly the opposite. They are doing something I have never heard of

19

before, except in the higher animals. They're using mimicry and imitation in immediate response to whatever is done to them – even though the things we give them to mimic are new each time!'

'Have Trillions got brains?' said Bem.

'I don't know. That's what worries me most.

Then Mina scampered in, cheeks glowing. 'Excuse me, Mr and Mrs Houghton, but I had to show you! My lovely bracelet!'

She held out her golden-brown wrist. On it there was a bracelet made of rosettes of glittering Trillions; a perfect pattern of flower shapes, repeated again and again, in glowing red, emerald and diamond white.

'Beautiful, Mina!' said Mrs Houghton. 'It must have taken you hours!'

'Oh, *they* did it! The Trillions! I made one pattern, and put it down on the ground in the middle of a whole heap of Trillions, and they just *did* it! You could watch them doing it! They just *formed* and I put sticky paper down on the patterns as they made them! Who are you?' Mina interrupted herself. She had noticed the stranger.

'This is Mr Blythe, Mina.'

'How do you do,' said Mina, politely. She shook hands uncertainly with him, then said – 'You're the space man! I saw your picture in a magazine! You went to the moon or somewhere in a spaceship!'

Scott and Bem exchanged looks. 'Blythe!' whispered Bem. 'Of course!'

'Why is your hair white? It wasn't white then. And you've got thinner,' burst out Mina.

Scott's father leaned forward in his chair. 'You are – were – Flight Commander Blythe . . . ?'

'Just Blythe now. And I've hung up my space unit. That's all over.'

Scott's father whistled quietly and said, 'Well . . . !'

'You've changed quite a lot,' said Scott's mother, quietly. 'I don't think I'd know you as the same man we all watched on TV that terrible time. You must have been through—'

'Well, that's all over,' repeated Blythe. 'And I'm not the same man. Not completely, anyhow.' He touched his face. Skin grafts, thought Scott. Skin grafts on his hands and face – and what else?

'Let me look at the bracelet again, Mina.'

She held it out to him, and asked, 'How old are you, Mister – I mean Commander – what you said?'

'That's not a polite thing to ask, Mina dear—' said Mrs Houghton. But for the first time, Blythe smiled. 'Forty-one. You can call me Icarus. It's simpler.'

There was an awkward silence while everyone waited for Mina to say, 'You look much older than that!'

But Mina said, 'That's a funny name, *Icarus*. I've never heard of anyone called *Icarus*. Is it a joke?'

Bem was just about to explain to Mina that Icarus was the man who tried to fly to the sun with wax wings, but the sun melted his wings and Icarus plunged to his death. Scott gave Bem a warning glance and Bem shut up.

Blythe carefully examined the bracelet without answering Mina. 'It's very pretty,' he said at last. 'You know what you should do now?'

Mina shook her head.'

'You should get them to make you a necklace to match!'

They watched Mina run from the room, delighted with the idea.

Bem said, 'You think Trillions are safe, then?'

'Safe enough to make pretty things for Mina. But the rest of us . . . I wonder what they mean to the rest of the world?'

Alone in his bedroom, Scott watched the 'forming' of Trillions through the low-power lenses of the microscope. They were easy to watch now; they moved no faster than ants, though sometimes, when they had 'work' to do, they were too quick to follow. He could not get used to them, could not get over them. He watched the outer, geared surfaces join and mesh, jostle and nudge, link and interlink, and imitate the simple pattern he had drawn on a sheet of paper. He watched one Trillion climb another, with tiny, shaking jerks as the teeth meshed; then the settling of the pyramid-like spike of one Trillion into the matching hole in the centre of another. He watched the mistakes the Trillions sometimes made – a pyramid Trillion would try to engage with another pyramid; discover the error; cog itself away; be replaced by the right sort of Trillion with a hollow centre.

After a time, he began to imagine he could hear the sounds the Trillions made. The little clicks as gear-tooth engaged with gear-tooth, the tiny sounds of falling as pyramid engaged in hold and locked there, the microscopic turnings and rollings and linkings and climbings.

At last he tired, got into bed and turned out the light. Now the room was almost dark, but he could not take his eyes from the dully glittering Trillions on the white paper by the window and still he could hear the sounds that did not exist – the little movements of the restless Trillions.

He slept, and dreamed Trillions. Do they *understand*?

He awoke to a world that was all Trillions. There were Trillions in Poland, Portugal, Pakistan; Trillions on the radio, in the newspapers, on TV. And in Harbourtown, there were helicopters in the sky, cars jamming the roads, motor cruisers rubbing the paint off each other's sides in the harbour, and, everywhere, men with cameras; still cameras, TV cameras, movie cameras.

The children went to school and found they could not get in: reporters and cameramen blocked the gates.

'Just a minute, sonny – what were you doing when the Trillions arrived?'

'What's your name? How old are you?'

'Who thought of calling them Trillions? You? Well, was it her, the little girl over there? What's your name, little girl? What's that? Louder! . . .'

'Were you scared? You weren't scared? Well, were you pleased? Both pleased and scared? Well, thank *you*, that's very helpful, I suppose . . .'

'What's your name? What's your age?'

They asked Bem questions like this. He answered stony-faced, staring straight back at the questioner.

'What's your name, sonny?'

'Sonny.'

'How old are you?'

'Twenty-seven. I'm a midget.'

'Be serious. What did you feel when you first saw the Trillions?'

'Thrillions.'

'Now listen, sonny, answer straight. Millions of people are watching you, you know . . .'

Bem stared blankly at the nearest TV camera then made himself squint. 'I can't see anyone,' he replied.

Mina showed the reporters her bracelet: the volley of flashbulbs almost blinded her.

But it was Scott the reporters wanted.

'You've talked with Mr Blythe, haven't you?'

'Yes. A little.'

'Did you know who he was? Did you know he was the spaceman?'

'Not at once, later—'

'Did you know he's here acting for the government – that he's one of our greatest authorities on space phenomenons?'

'Phenomen*a*,' Bem interrupted. 'The plural of phenomenon is phenomena.'

'Get that kid out of here. Now listen, Scott, don't go away . . .'

Miss Wolfe and Mr Clark, teachers, tried to get the children into the school. They tried for half an hour, then gave up. 'No school today!' they shouted, over the crowd. 'You can all go home! Go home, do you hear?' But Mina had found someone else to show her bracelet to, and Scott was in the clutches of a hard, blonde, tanned girl reporter in an expensive suede jacket decorated with three expensive cameras.

'Tell me, Scott,' she whispered – or it felt like being whispered to, in spite of the noise – 'Tell me *all about yourself*. Now, your father: what does he do?' She made her eyes pop open wide as she waited for the answer.

'Builds boats. Runs the marina here.'

'Boats! A *wonderful* way of life!' The eyes popped again. 'And your *mother*, Scott, what does she do?'

'Runs the house. All sorts of things.'

'What *sort* of things, Scott?'

'Oh, she does pottery and textile designs. As a freelance.'

'Oh, an *artist*. So your mother is an *artist* . . . ?'

She gave him the same sort of feeling you get when you go to pick up a jar of jam and someone has left it sticky. Scott escaped but was caught straight away by an elderly reporter with a tape recorder and a bright purple face, glistening with sweat.

This reporter jabbed questions at Scott as if they were friendly punches from a flyweight boxer. They didn't hurt but you could not escape them.

'So why was Mr Blythe in your home? What did he say about Trillions? What did he reply? What did he mean by that? Was he looking worried? Well, how was he looking? What do you mean, normal? How do you know he looked normal if this was the first time you met him? So he was looking a little anxious? You said a little anxious? Anxious was the word you used? Now, why do you think he was anxious? What do *you* think anyone's got to be anxious about?'

'All right, that's enough,' a voice said in Scott's ear. It was 'Icarus' Blythe. 'Come with me. No more questions. Come on, Scott.'

Scott was delighted to find himself being towed away. 'In here,' said Blythe, pushing open the back door of the school house. It was empty inside, of course. They sat down, each in a desk, and were silent for a minute.

'Wow,' said Blythe. 'I thought I was over all this.'

'You mean, after that moonshot? All the reporters?'

'Yes, all the reporters. It's a funny thing: you can't stop yourself answering them. And the more people there are, the more answers they get out of you. It's catching. Everyone gets the questions and answers disease, everyone behaves the same way.'

'I know, I felt like that. You don't want to, but you have to,' said Scott. He yawned. He was blazing with excitement yet numb with lack of sleep. He felt like two people having a quarrel.

'Didn't you sleep well last night?' asked Blythe.

'Oh yes, fine. Well, I slept all right. It's just that I couldn't get to sleep. I'd been looking at the Trillions again, at low power. You know, the microscope. And couldn't stop thinking about them.'

'What do you think about them?' asked Blythe sharply. Then he laughed, and said, 'Just like a reporter.'

'I don't – I don't know. I don't understand why you ask me, my opinions aren't worth—'

'Nobody's opinion is worth anything so far. That's why I ask you. You probably know as much about Trillions as anyone else in the world. Why assume that I know any more than you?'

'But you are a Professor or a Flight Commander or . . . I mean, you're *qualified*.'

Blythe stood up and stretched, then sat down again. 'I am Icarus – the one who got his wings singed. All the other titles mean nothing.' Scott stared at him, expressionlessly.

'Scott, once, not so long ago, I was the greatest expert in the world on a certain surface of the Moon. I was the greatest expert because I was the only expert. No one had been there but me. And do you know what all my expert knowledge amounted to?'

Scott shook his head.

'It amounted to this. I was alone, my suit was over-heating, I was feeling a bit sick, and the Moon wasn't made of green cheese. That's what being the greatest expert in the world meant then. And that's very much the position with Trillions. We're world experts, both of us – and a hundred per cent ignorant. So tell me what you think!'

'If I do, will you tell me what *you* think?' Scott answered.

'Yes, certainly.' He met Scott's eyes and added, 'I mean it.'

'All right. I think Trillions are invaders of some sort from another planet. Or from space. I think they're intelligent. Probably more intelligent than . . . than bees, say . . .'

'Why bees? Why did you pick on bees? Are bees intelligent?'

'I suppose because Trillions can do all sorts of things that you could call "clever". So can bees. But is it "cleverness" or is it just instinct, or habit, or something that just developed over millions of years?'

'Bees make choices,' said Blythe.

'I know. They decide whether they're going to stand guard duty, or fan the hive to ventilate it, or look after the queen bee, or go and collect pollen, or work on the honey-combs. And they can give each other messages. Instinct or intelligence?'

'You seem to know a lot about bees,' said Blythe, raising an eyebrow.

'It's all instinct with bees, I suppose,' said Scott, ignoring the raised eyebrow. 'At least, that's what they teach us.'

'And now we have Trillions. Things the world has never seen before. "Clever" things, or things with instincts developed for situations that are never met with on our planet. For heaven's sake!' he broke off, 'Let's move!'

A face had appeared at the window, then more faces, all behind cameras. Scott and Icarus Blythe took seats right against the wall where no one could see them.

Icarus leaned down and scooped together the bright dust that had collected along the skirting of the wall. 'Look,' he said, holding out the palm of his hand, loaded with dust, for Scott to inspect. 'Trillions! A handful of Trillions. You and I look at them and wonder about them . . .

'Do you think,' he continued, 'that they are looking right back at us?'

Outside in the streets, there was a new commotion. The morning editions of the evening newspapers had arrived. As fast as the men and boys in the vans could unload, hands grabbed. The headlines screamed—

TRILLIONS!
WORLD SCIENTISTS PROBE
INVADERS FROM SPACE
FRIEND – OR DEADLY FOE?

Bem, Mina and Panda shared the only copy they could get with three other children. The front-page pictures showed magnified Trillions like great gem stones, and a street scene in Harbourtown West.

'Turn over!' said Bem, impatiently.

'"WORLD REACTION TO OTHER-WORLD INVADERS". Stop there a minute . . .' Frowning, he read the short paragraphs, each headed with the name of a capital city. Moscow, Paris, Rome, New York, London . . .

'They don't say anything!' said Panda, crossly.

'They don't know anything,' answered Bem. 'That's why.'

'Ooo! Look! Me!' squeaked Mina. And there, sure enough, she was. The photographer had caught her at the moment when she held out her bracelet. The caption read, 'THE TRUST OF A LITTLE CHILD'.

'Urggh!' said Bem.

'*I am* a little child,' said Mina. 'Quite little. And anyhow, why shouldn't I trust them?' She admired the bracelet on her arm. 'They're only Trillions,' she said.

Next day, however, there was real news in the newspapers: the Trillions had 'formed' in a new and sinister way.

Harbourtown was once again the first place where it

happened. Two local youths, whose hobby was skin-diving, reported. 'There's something strange down there in the water. Something huge. Like a – a *fortress*, all made of Trillions.'

Their underwater photographs showed great untidy blocks with holes like windows, dark towers and turrets looming in the dim waters; caves like great entrance halls, black and terrifying, that the swimmers dared not penetrate. Looking at the photographs, 'fortress' seemed as good a word as any for the structure. But a child playing in the sand with bucket and spade could have done better than the Trillions . . .

Very soon, there were more Trillion structures – a vast 'aeroplane' in a Vietnam jungle – a 'factory' (or was it a 'battleship'?) near Houston, Texas – a tower rather like an enormous gun barrel in Holland – and many others.

'These structures,' Scott said to Icarus, 'they simply don't make sense. What good are they? What could the Trillions *use* them for?'

'The more you look at them the less sense they make,' said Icarus, prodding a newspaper photograph of a 'fortress' in Japan.

Scott shrugged and stared at the picture in silence. He found himself remembering Blythe's words – 'Do you think they are looking right back at us?' The thought made him shiver.

'They haven't got eyes,' he said at last.

'What was that?'

'Trillions haven't got eyes,' said Scott. 'Nor anything that looks like eyes. How could they look at us?'

'Perhaps the whole Trillion construction is an optical system. All those jewel-like facets may add up to an "eye", just as a fly's eye is made up of thousands of lenses.'

'And brains . . . I wonder about the brains,' said Scott. 'Bees have brains, but they run their lives by a bigger brain – the brain of the hive.'

'Good description,' said Blythe. 'Mind you, human beings do much the same thing. We act as single, individual persons, but we also act as groups, or mobs, or races, or whole nations.'

'Suppose they do have brains. What have they been thinking? Did they think of coming to our planet – or just arrive by accident?'

'And when they make patterns, when they "form", are they thinking – or just behaving?' said Blythe.

'I suppose the most important question is, what do they want?' said Scott, speaking slowly. 'What do they hope for here?'

'Assuming they can hope or think at all,' Blythe reminded him.

Scott thought for a long minute, then looked up at Blythe and said, 'You're worried, aren't you? You're afraid that they can think, and they've come here for a purpose.'

'Yes, of course I'm worried. I am one of the people who has got to try and find out what Trillions are, what they mean to us, how we must treat them. You see, it's not simply a matter of scientific facts. It's more like . . . well, it's like waking up in the middle of the night because you've heard a noise downstairs. So you go downstairs. The noise is coming from the kitchen. You open the door, and there's

31

this enormous dog. He's got great white teeth. When you go near to him, he snarls at you – but wags his tail at the same time!'

Scott laughed.

'What do you do with a dog like that?' Blythe said. 'Throw him into the cold? But that's cruel. And anyhow, he might bite you. Give him food? But do you really want an enormous dog in your house from then on?'

'*So* what *do* you do?' said Scott.

There was a short, dry, rattling sound, like rice being thrown against a window. The man and the boy scrambled to their feet. There was a cloud over the blue sky – a cloud that glittered and twinkled in its depths.

The light, dry rattling sounded again against the window pane.

'More Trillions,' said Blythe.

And now the streets were suddenly filled by another invasion. This time, it was the Army. While the Trillions rained down from a clear sky, the streets of Harbourtown West became blocked with trucks carrying steel-helmeted men, with staff cars, with soldiers carrying walkie-talkies, with white-gaitered military policemen directing traffic, with special road signs. There was even an Army helicopter overhead making such a din that no one on the ground could hear all the orders and counter-orders and directions and commands that the soldiers gave each other.

Mina soon got herself a soldier. His name was Billy. He was over six feet tall and had freckles and bright yellow hair.

He called Mina 'little lady' and carried her about on his shoulder until an officer told him not to.

'What are you going to do about the Trillions, Billy?' Mina asked. She looked very pretty with her necklace and bracelet.

'That's a good question, little lady,' said Billy, not answering it. His voice was deep and vague. When he spoke, he sounded rather like a cow mooing.

'Do you like Trillions?' said Mina, flashing her eyes and her bracelet at him.

'Don't know one way or the other, little lady,' said Billy. 'No orders yet.'

'I bet you're stronger than the Trillions,' said Mina.

'Could be,' said the soldier, screwing up his eyes and sticking out his chin. 'Could be,' he repeated, in a tough voice.

'I bet you're stronger than all the Trillions in the world!' said Mina, squeezing his hand. 'I bet you could smash them and bash them and mash them and hash them—'

'Could be,' said Billy, nodding his head menacingly.

'Well, I bet you could,' said Mina, adoringly.

Billy looked around him, saw no officers, and put Mina back on his shoulders.

'Vroom! Ker-Bang!' she shouted. 'Pow! Bam! Splat!'

In Scott Houghton's house, the Army seemed to have formed a sort of headquarters. There were officers and soldiers everywhere, under the command of an Army Major.

'Glad to meet you, sir,' said the Major, 'And not only

glad: honoured.' He pumped Blythe's hand up and down vigorously and stuck out his chin, just like Billy.

Blythe mumbled something but couldn't get his hand away.

'Your achievement, sir,' the Major went on, 'was an inspiration to . . .' Suddenly he dropped Blythe's hand and yelled 'Hey, SOLDIER! Yes, YOU! Over here at the double!'

Billy the soldier sheepishly put Mina down, and doubled over 'SIR!' he mooed, saluting smartly.

'Your mission here, soldier, is a military mission,' began the Major, sticking out his chin still further. 'MILITARY, you understand? At ease soldier,' grated the Major. 'Stand by to run messages.'

Billy stood at ease. The Major scratched his grizzled grey hair under his field cap and started again.

'My duty is plain enough. In fact, it's all here in Orders,' he said, tapping a leather folder significantly with a large, clean finger. 'My duty is to protect the citizens of this town, this country, this nation, against their foes. Sounds simple enough, but is it?' The Major stopped dramatically and stared into Blythe's face with rounded eyes. 'Trouble is, we don't know what we're up against. You follow me?'

'I follow you,' said Blythe patiently.

'I want some lemonade,' said Mina, and skipped out of the room.

'The Trillions . . .' said Blythe.

'Yes, the Trillions,' said the Major. 'Now we've dealt with the lemonade question, perhaps we could talk about the Trillions. Sir,' he said, making himself look soldierly again by puffing out his chest and thrusting forward his chin, 'I've got just one simple question to put to you – and I need hardly say that a great deal depends on your answer . . .

'These Trillions: are they Friend – or Foe? Do we bless them – or do we BLAST THEM OFF THE FACE OF THE EARTH!'

'Guess which he'd rather do!' whispered Bem to Scott.

Blythe took a deep, slow breath before he replied.

'Major,' he said, 'I don't know what fire-power you've got here—'

''38's, 75's, napalm and all the usual small arms,' interrupted the Major, happily.

Blythe lifted a hand. 'Major, as I was about to say, I don't know what weapons you've got – any more than I know if Trillions are friend or foe – but I do know one thing. I found it out last night. Scott,' he said, 'Would you get me a hammer and something to use as an anvil? Thanks . . .

'Now, while Scott gets them, I want you, Major, to pick out just one Trillion from this collection here. Give him the saucer, Bem.' Bem took the saucerful of Trillions he kept by the microscope and held it out before the Major. The Major took one.

'Put it in this,' said Blythe, opening out a white paper envelope. The Major dropped in the Trillion. Scott came back with the hammer and an anvil in the shape of a rusty old anchor blade. He looked at Bem as if to say 'What is happening?' Bem shrugged.

'Now, Major, you talk about blasting Trillions off the

face of the earth, and smashing them and so on. And you are a man of action. Well, let's see you go into action and smash just one single Trillion. Here's a Trillion. I place it, in its envelope, on the anvil. Here's the anvil. And here's the hammer. Right?'

Uncertainly, the Major took the hammer. He pushed a finger on to the envelope and the little bump of the Trillion showed through. He took aim with the hammer and brought it down hard. The little bump was flat. The Major handed the hammer to Blythe and said, 'Well?'

'Look inside the envelope.'

The Major looked.

'It's smashed! Smithereens! Beat into powder!' he laughed loudly. 'Well, there you are, Sir!'

'Now come over to the microscope, Major. Is it set up, Bem? Focused? Good. Sit down, Major. Take a look.'

The Major silently peered through the microscope. A minute passed. 'Nothing to report,' he said. 'Not a thing!'

'Nothing?' said Blythe. 'You're sure?'

Bem and Scott looked at each other.

'Nothing. Just stuff like powdered glass.'

'Right! So you have smashed a Trillion. But now watch this . . .'

He increased the magnification of the microscope, used the fine focus, and invited the Major to look. 'See anything?'

The Major peered into the microscope for some time in silence. Then looked up and said, 'Strange. Thought I saw something move!'

'Keep looking, Major,' said Blythe.

The Major kept looking, sometimes dabbing impatiently at the fine-focus wheel.

'Have trouble keeping them in focus, Major?'

'Damn things seem to be moving all the time. Something wrong with the microscope?'

'I'll make a little adjustment. Bem, where's the high-power objective? Thanks . . .'

He screwed the highest-power lens into place, carefully re-focused and invited the Major to look.

As he looked, the Major's neck seemed to swell in his collar, as if it were a red rubber ring being blown up, puff by puff. 'Blast them!' he roared, swivelling his head to glare at Blythe, 'Blast them! Know what they're doing? The broken bits are meshing together! Climbing! Gearing! *That Trillion I smashed has become more Trillions!*'

The expression on his face was so outraged, so childishly peevish, that Scott knew he would have to laugh. The arrival of General Hartman saved him.

The door was thrown open by Billy. He suddenly looked a soldier.

'SAH!' yelled Billy. He raised his right knee and brought the heel of his boot down with a crashing thump on Mrs Houghton's polished floor. He tucked his chin into his Adam's apple, braced his shoulders back so hard that his whole body quivered, and yelled, 'General Hartman – SAH!'

General Hartman strode into the room, stopped exactly in the centre and said, very quietly, 'At ease.'

'SAH! screeched Billy.

'Major?' said General Hartman.

'SIR!' bellowed the Major, standing rigidly to attention. Mrs Houghton came in, glancing anxiously at the mark Billy's heel left in the floor, then at the General.

'Major, introduce us,' said the General.

'This is Mrs Houghton, General, who has kindly allowed—'

'Mrs Houghton. Honoured. Grateful.' The General extended a hand that might have been part of a machine. Scott and Bem also shook for a second the dry, hard hand that exerted no pressure whatsoever.

Mina came in with her glass of lemonade. 'This is Mina,' said Mrs Houghton, rather faintly.

'Charmed. Pretty. Thank you,' said the General, taking the glass of lemonade from her and draining it. Mina stared at him round-eyed, said 'But! . . .' and shut up.

For there was very little you could say to the General. He stood precisely five feet five inches tall. Every inch was covered in expensive material. His cavalry boots were of a leather so old and beautiful that the various shades of mahogany seemed to be lit from within. His cavalry breeches were of a light tan whipcord in which every thread seemed to be formed into ranks and all the ranks stood at attention. His tunic, of a much darker brown, had pleated pockets that might have been carved from a hard, dark wood. His medal ribbons, straps, belts, buckles, tabs, collar and tie seemed so permanently perfect that it was possible to imagine that the single drop of moisture that had fallen from Mina's glass on his lapel would shortly sizzle and evaporate itself, out of shame.

Even his hair and skin seemed to be made of some costly inhuman material. The grey hairs were perfectly grey, the white hairs were perfectly white, and each colour was sharply divided from the other – white at the temples, grey elsewhere. His eyes were blue marbles made of the finest and most highly polished glass, while his skin was of that beautiful, parchment-like leather found only in the suitcases of, millionaires.

'Major,' continued the General, 'Want your report, now. Outside. My compliments, Mrs Houghton, and truly grateful. Come.'

He left the room, and everyone seemed suddenly able to breathe.

'Wow . . !' said Bem.

Scott looked at Blythe. He was fingering a scar on his cheek and staring at nothing.

'First that rather stupid Major,' said Mrs Houghton weakly, 'And now . . .'

'Now, the General. General Hartman. Now *him*,' said Blythe. 'It would have to be *him* . . .' Blythe suddenly looked ill. Scott felt sorry for him.

'Well, I'd rather have the General in charge than that Major,' said Scott.

'The Major is moronic,' said Bem. 'Moron Major. Major Disaster.'

'But the General – well, he's quite something,' said Scott. 'Isn't he, Icarus?' The nickname slipped out.

Blythe appeared not to have heard for a moment. Then he stopped fingering his scar and said, 'Oh, the General. General Hartman. General Hartman, Scott, is as you said

– quite something. Quite something. "Heartless Hartman", no less . . . I think he is the most dangerous man I've ever met.'

Mrs Houghton smiled and said, 'Surely, Mr Blythe, you don't really mean that?'

'I do.'

'But why?'

'Because he never has doubts. And he always gets action.'

'But I still don't see—'

'Suppose, Mrs Houghton, that the General was absolutely wrong about something very important.'

Chapter Four

The General was efficient. The General was a leader. The General was an organizer. And the General was everywhere.

Under his command, Harbourtown West became overnight a barracks and everyone in the town a conscript. Suddenly, it seemed, you could no longer park your car outside the library – the space was sealed off with white ropes and filled with brown Army vehicles. So you tried the little square, where there were parking meters. But now there were never any meters vacant – the spaces that had been yours were painted with new yellow lines and the meters themselves had their heads in bags marked 'OUT OF ORDER'.

There seemed suddenly to be quite a number of loud-speakers in the town. They blossomed overnight, growing on lamp posts and telegraph poles. Music came out of them but also mysterious messages: 'B company personnel report HQ oblique Three Seven I will repeat that HQ oblique THUR-REE SEV-ENN. Out.'

Everyone said, 'Well, I suppose there is good reason for it.'

Or suppose you were Billy, Mina's soldier. Billy played the guitar. For years now, Billy and his friends had practised whenever they could. Wherever the Army sent him, Billy always found friends to play the guitar with. In Harbourtown West, he met a young man called Bert, a garage mechanic.

One night, Bert was walking along through the sleeping streets after a guitar session with Billy – it was three in the morning – when a huge shape moved out of the shadows and a hard voice said, 'Halt! Who goes there?' It was a soldier in a glinting steel helmet and a wicked looking rifle.

Bert was so frightened he dropped his guitar case. The guitar case made a hollow sound as it hit the pavement – but a far worse sound came from within the case. Bert knew what it was: it was his guitar, the guitar, the finest and most expensive guitar in Harbourtown West, breaking its neck with the shock of the fall.

'—!' said Bert, and instinctively lunged forward towards the guitar.

The soldier jabbed with his rifle and broke one of Bert's teeth.

Bert must have gone a little mad. He kept pushing the soldier away from the place where the guitar lay, then kicking and punching. The soldier, who had not meant to hurt anyone, had to defend himself. Bert spent the night in jail.

Next morning, Bert appeared in the court of justice and gave his evidence as clearly as he could through a swollen mouth. The Chief Magistrate of the three, an old man in a thoroughly bad temper, kept shuffling his papers impatiently and muttering 'Can't *hear*. Can't *hear*.' The Clerk of the Court barked 'SPEAK UP!' and Bert mumbled louder. Then the sentry was called to give evidence.

But at this moment, a soldier's voice bellowed 'SAH!' and the General was striding up the centre of the Court, and Bert and the soldier were quite forgotten. Could the General be granted the privilege of saying a few words? The magistrate supposed so, but it was most irregular. Could the General ask the Court to allow the military forces to take what action was necessary? The Court hummed and hawed. Might the General remind the Court that the soldier was under military discipline and it was only proper that he be tried by the military authorities? The Court uneasily agreed. Could the General draw the Court's attention to the very serious nature of the situation in Harbourtown West and ask all possible cooperation in maintaining discipline, both civil and military, during the present emergency? The Court was not quite clear as to what the General meant either by 'cooperation' or 'emergency', but supposed there was no objection. Might the General approach the magistrates and speak to them privately?

The magistrates obviously disliked this idea, but there seemed no way of stopping the General. He was already marching towards the Bench. They surrendered to the determined, spotless, disciplined figure approaching them and listened while he spoke to them so quietly that no one else could hear.

Then the Chief Magistrate growled 'Case dismissed!' The soldier saluted: a Sergeant standing near him told him he shouldn't have done: the soldier turned red, thumped clumsily down the stairs and was gone. The General bowed to the magistrates, about-turned and left the court, his heels echoing on the floor. The clerk of the Court shouted, 'Order in court!' quite needlessly, for no one had made a sound. The affair was over.

Yet no one could stop talking about it. Some people took it very badly. Mr Houghton was furious and his wife uneasy.

'What does he mean, that General, walking into our courthouse and running our affairs for us?'

'You'd think we had a military government . . .'

A day or so after, everyone had cooled down. 'Well,' they said, 'There must be a good reason for it. That General seems to know what he's doing . . .'

But Icarus Blythe, white-faced, would not discuss the matter at all.

'I suppose there must be a good reason for it,' said Scott uncertainly.

Bem said, '*What* good reason?'

'Well, the General's idea of cleaning up the place. The Trillions are everywhere. All over the place. Someone's got to get rid of them. It may as well be us. It might even be fun, going around with a little barrow and brooms and shovels—'

'Fun . . !' said Bem.

'Well, there's our barrow,' said Scott. And there it was indeed. An Army-brown metal wheelbarrow with hooks on the side to carry the Broom (1) Army Issue, and Shovels (2) Army Issue.

'G stroke One Eleven stroke A Two, Double-you Dee,' said Panda, reading out the number stencilled on the side of the barrow. 'Proper old hot-rod.'

'They say we've got to make up teams,' said Scott.

'You make up a team,' replied Bem. 'You're the leader. You're the biggest and oldest. Make up a team.' He made a small rude noise.

'All right, I will!' said Scott, jumping to his feet. 'You, me, Panda—'

'—And Mina,' said Panda.

'Why Mina? For goodness' sake, why her?'

'Because if anyone can find a way of getting us out of pushing a barrow – Mina can!'

'All right, all right!' said Bem gloomily. 'Barrows . . . Shovels . . . *Mina* . . .'

The streets were filled with barrows, boys and girls. The barrows squeaked and thumped and clanged. The boys yelled, bumped barrows and dropped spades on people's feet. The girls screamed 'Don't!' and 'Stop it!' or just stood bending forward from the hips, shouting gossip into each other's faces.

Yet, slowly, order came from this chaos. Someone discovered that the only way to keep his team together was to invent a rallying call: someone else made a rival call; and soon, every team had its own cry.

So while one boy shouted, 'TRILLY-willy-willions!' you could hear another farther down the road hooting, 'Yodel-AY-EE-TEE!' like a Swiss shepherd. Scott's call was quite simply, 'HI HO TRILLIONS!'

Quite soon, the teams actually went to work. You crashed your barrow against everyone else's, made your way to any place where there were drifts of Trillions – Trillions were everywhere – and shovelled them up. The shovels made a good loud scraping noise, the Trillions were clean and light and easy to swing into the barrow (the smaller children used plastic buckets and spades) so everyone was kept busy. When the barrow was something like full, you shouted your rallying cry and hurtled the barrow along the road to the dumping ground, crashing into any other barrows you met on the way. Finally, you tipped out the load of Trillions on to the fast-growing heap.

Soon this heap became a pyramid of considerable size and some soldiers constructed a raised walk from planks and steel tubing. This made the tipping more amusing – it was quite dramatic to trundle your barrow along the echoing planks, then stop with a jerk – thrust the handles up and forward – and watch the glistening, twinkling Trillions fall away from you, in a glittering curve, to spill over the top of the pyramid. Some children jumped in on top of the pile, whooping with joy, but the soldiers soon stopped this.

Meanwhile, a whole team of soldiers was bulldozing a site right beside the Trillions dump. This was worth watching. The giant yellow bulldozers chuntered and thundered, screamed and yelped. Tons of earth were pushed this way and that by vast, curved blades, their steel polished by the work. Nonchalant soldiers perched on top of these yellow monsters, pulling levers, baring biceps, lighting cigarettes and twisting the peaks of their caps into rakish shapes.

'What are you doing?' Panda asked one of them.

'Trillion trap!' shouted the soldier. 'Make a big hole, then a special machine to get rid of the Trillions. General's orders. Now stand clear, sweetheart!'

'Special machine?' said Bem to Scott. 'What can he mean, special machine?'

'What can he mean, special machine!' sang Mina, prancing about to the rhythm of the words. 'Special machine! What can he mean!'

Bem scowled. Scott decided to have another talk with Icarus.

Icarus was always surprisingly easy to find and surprisingly easy to talk to. Before Scott had come to accept Blythe – before Mr Blythe had become Icarus to Scott and his friends – this had been a puzzle. After all, Icarus Blythe was an important and famous man who had been sent by the government to examine and report on a matter of world importance – the coming of the Trillions. Telephones rang and voices asked for Mr Blythe. Big cars whisked Mr Blythe to airports. Military and civil aircraft carried Mr Blythe to London, Washington, Paris, anywhere. Yet somehow he managed to return frequently to Harbourtown, where he spent most of his time in the public library. Scott asked him why. Icarus pointed to a sign that read, NO TALKING.

'Oh, I'm sorry,' said Scott.

'I didn't mean you,' said Icarus, smiling slightly. 'I meant *them*. I escape them here.'

Scott did not like to ask the next question, but asked it all the same. 'Why?' he said. 'What have you got against them? Which them?'

'I mean the people who don't know,' said Icarus, 'and the people who think they know. I mean most people who ask questions, and everyone who asks the wrong questions.'

He had raised his voice. Now, he pointed again at the notice; gave a small smile; and said, 'Let's get out of here. I need a walk. And you've got something on your mind.'

They walked, fast but without purpose. Scott was on Icarus's blind side. He could look up at the expressionless face and study the small scars round the blinded eye, the tight mouth with the firm-set creases at its corners, the hand that had been broken and repaired. He felt as if he were spying but continued to observe. Soon he found himself running out of breath: Icarus was walking faster and faster, with no apparent effort. Scott set himself to keep up and thought, 'This man looks like an athlete and a college professor and a soldier and an invalid and a success and a failure . . . I don't understand him at all.'

Suddenly Icarus stopped. 'It's the reporters I can't stand. Do you know what "human interest" means, Scott? I'm "human interest". So are you, but not so much as that little girl, Mina. I am "human interest" because I was once a spaceman, a pioneer, a hero. I went up there and the whole world watched with one eye and ate TV snacks. And then things went wrong up there and they forgot all about the snacks. They watched with both eyes – watched like hawks – when things went wrong. I suppose all sorts of dear old people said all sorts of dear old prayers and all the children said "Wow!" and "Gee!" and "Gosh!" And I suppose not one person in a million saw what it was all about . . .'

'What was it all about?' said Scott at last.

'Whatever it was, it wasn't "human interest". It wasn't about a man in space, or what his wife thought about it, or whether his mother worried, or how he ate his meals—'

'Or what happened when the heat shield failed and you got your – your—'

'You're just the same as the rest, Scott. You want to hear the gory details, the "human interest", don't you?'

'No. Yes, I suppose so. But not so much as I want to understand what you are talking about.' Scott found himself losing his temper. The words rushed out. 'You ought to try and explain! It's not fair, doing what you do. You just complain and sound bitter and start saying something and then shut yourself up and then criticize *me*! . . .'

Blythe, for the first time since Scott had known him, suddenly looked human and ordinary – and ashamed. When he began talking again, even his voice had changed. It was urgent, interested, warm.

'You're right. Absolutely right. I apologize, and now I'm going to explain. And first, I'll tell you why I am explaining to you, and not to anyone else. It's because you have an open mind. It's because you are *not an adult* . . .'

He seemed unable to continue with this thought and started again.

'Scott,' he said, 'tell me what would happen if your father lost all his business. No money, nothing. What would happen?'

'I don't know. I suppose he would have to begin all over again – find ways of raising money, paying his debts—'

'Fine. He would start all over again – but he would start along the same road, wouldn't he? He wouldn't say to himself, 'Well, I am completely lost. I am not *me* any more.' Right?'

'All right.'

'But now take a child. A very young child, with a smiling mother and a kind father. They take that child, put it in the family car, drive out to a desert. Then the mother, still smiling, throws the child out of the car. The father, still smiling, begins to drive off. The child tries to follow. It's in pain, it's crying, it's hysterical, screaming – it tries to follow the car. But the car just keeps going and the mother keeps smiling and the father turns round to wave. And then the car gathers speed and is gone. The child is alone in a strange place. What happens to that child, Scott?'

'It must die. It will strave or go mad or . . . look, I don't understand, I don't like this idea about the child—'

'Does it frighten you, Scott?'

'All right, it frightens me. Is that what you are after?'

'No, I want to explain to you. Scott, just once or twice in your life, you have felt what the child in the desert must feel. Perhaps you had no reason to feel it, but you felt it all the same and you are young enough to remember it. Right?'

'Yes . . . Once I got locked in the tool shed. After a time I knew I was going to die there. I just knew it was the end.

That was after I had finished screaming and yelling . . . It was when I was quiet that I *knew* . . .'

Scott shook himself.

'And it still makes you shudder. Later, Scott, you will remember that time without shuddering. You will remember it as something that happens to small boys if they are not careful in garden sheds. By then, you will be like any other adult. You will have learned all kinds of rules and ways of doing things, thinking about things, just as I did when I was being trained for space.

'Then one day, you *are* in space. In a capsule. You know everything there is to know about what you are doing. You know that whatever happens, there is a button to push, a procedure, a course of action. You know you are in danger. You know you may die – but your training covers that too. More buttons. In case of death, push button B.

'Suddenly, things go wrong. The ship goes mad, it's spinning, tumbling, throwing you face-first into all those familiar buttons. You feel yourself being broken, pieces of you smashed. But all the time, there is a calm voice inside you. Deep down, you still know *what to do*. It's all in the book.'

'Then it turns out though everything is smashed and broken, including you, the panic is over. You are alive and alone. Alone, Scott, really *alone* . . .

'But you make yourself get used to it. The hours pass and you learn to live with it. Your watch tells you that a morning has passed, or a day, or a night: they all look the same up there, you just have to believe your watch. I got very fond of my watch, Scott . . .' He showed Scott his wristwatch;

there was a curved scar in the metal of the case. 'To me, this watch was humankind. It ticked. It was alive. I used to hold it up to my ear and just listen to it, ticking and ticking.

He paused. Scott suddenly saw a vision, like a photograph appearing in his mind, of the solitary figure in the space capsule. The figure was like a huge, elaborate, insect-like toy. It had a glinting, glassy, bulbous head. Its skin was of metallic silver material. Outside its body were veins – tubes and pipes and wires. But inside the glass-globe head there was a human face, in pain. And from one of the silvery armtubes there dangled a human hand, a brown hand with hairs on the back of it, nails on each finger tip and human warmth inside it. The hand moved uneasily and blood dripped from one finger.

'That loneliness . . .' Icarus went on. 'I got used to it. They say you can get used to anything, I don't know. But I got used to my own loneliness after a day or two – or three, I don't know how long. But then, Scott, something came up that I hadn't been expecting. I got used to my own loneliness, but I found there was another sort of loneliness I couldn't get used to. *Its* loneliness! The loneliness of space itself!

'And that's when the nightmare really began. I don't know how to describe this, Scott, but I'll try. They tell you that space is emptiness, nothingness – the void. They suggest that space, empty space, is something negative. I found out that it's not! Space *lives*, Scott, Nothingness, emptiness, has a life all its own.'

They kept walking.

'I found,' said Icarus, 'that space has got its own . . .

atmosphere. That's a silly word to use! Atmosphere is just what outer space *hasn't* got. But you know what I mean. When I look back and remember space, I can almost smell it, feel it, touch it.'

'What sort of atmosphere had space?' asked Scott.

Icarus replied with one word. 'Alien.'

'Alien?'

'Alone, Apart, Foreign. Unlike anything known to man. Alien.'

'Alien good, or alien bad?'

It took a long time for Blythe to reply. At last he said, 'That's the puzzle. That's the mystery. How can you tell? How can you begin to understand something completely alien? Good, bad, I don't know. All I know is – alien.'

Icarus limped away, fast. Scott was left wondering.

He stayed wondering all day and continued wondering in bed that night.

'We'll never understand, never!' Icarus had said. What had he meant? Could you 'understand' a honey bee? Perhaps he had meant, 'We'll never get through, establish contact, be useful to each other.' Honey bees were useful to humans, so humans made themselves useful to honey bees. Give a hive, take some honey.

The trouble was that Trillions had nothing to offer us and we had nothing to offer them.

And yet, thought Scott, Trillions 'try'. They imitate, make shapes, appear to want to play our game. While all we do is talk about them, write about them, make big newspaper and TV stories about them. Trillions try: we don't.

Scott got into bed and looked around him. There was a dusting of Trillions on the window sill and a powdering of them on the floor. He got out of bed and opened the window. The window ledge was coated inches deep with Trillions. He scooped them up with his hands and put them on the sheet of drawing paper on his table. Soon he had a big heap of Trillions. He sat on the edge of his bed staring at them.

Aliens.

There was a scrawling mark on the paper. Some Trillions were busily beginning to reproduce the mark. Scott watched for a little while, sighed and went back to his bed. The Trillions puzzled him, Icarus puzzled him. He got into bed and turned out the light.

In the darkness, he thought he could just hear the very faint scratch and scrabble of the Trillions as they linked and climbed over each other. Scott turned over in bed and tried to ignore the tiny sounds.

Ah! he thought, I am falling asleep. Gratefully, he allowed the familiar fall-asleep processes of his brain to take over. Colours, picture, snatches of rhyme came into his head from nowhere. He welcomed them. Soon the screen of his brain would go dark and he would sleep.

Charlie Chaplin went to France

To teach the natives how to dance said his brain. Children skipping. Rope twirls, skinny legs jump.

First he did the rumba
Then he did the kicks
Then he did the turnabout
Then he did the splits

said his brain. But Scott found himself replying, 'No!' He turned over again and his eyes opened. What was wrong?

'Kicks' and 'splits' did not rhyme.

He started another rhyme.

A,B,C,D,E,F,G
That's what teacher said to me

ABC! Teacher! He sat up in bed, wide awake; switched on the light and went to work.

It took him a week to teach the Trillions their ABC. A week that seemed endless. A week that made Scott think that if the Trillions had any intelligence, they were very clever at hiding it.

His method was simple. He wrote an A and the Trillions 'formed' to imitate it. When they were half-way to completing their imitation, he wrote more A's. This confused their purpose. Some Trillions would break away from the A already half-formed to enlist in the armies making new A's. They became so confused that often A's would be formed without the Trillions following a pattern. Eventually, he could write one single small A, watch too many Trillions queueing to form it, scatter the heap and stand back: within minutes, there would be small A's everywhere.

The B's, C's, D's – all the letters of the alphabet. By the end of the week, they could form words. Scott would write WORD once: the Trillions would swarm around the writing: then disperse themselves into groups to make WORD WORD WORD WORD WORD WORD WORD, all over the floor.

At this stage, Scott collected more Trillions from the streets and tried to make them perform the same trick.

They could not at first. They had to blend themselves into the mass of trained Trillions. Then they could perform.

'So my trained Trillions are different from just any old Trillions,' thought Scott. 'They can learn. The trouble is, they have no idea of the meaning of what they've learned. They can write WORD without knowing what a Word is. How can I teach them that?'

Chapter Five

School routines were broken up. School in the morning: Trillions in the afternoon. Each day Scott's team spent three hours in the noisy streets, where the loud speakers were always pouring out their mixture of soothing music and barked commands and the trucks roared by and the soldiers worked at nothing in particular and the journalists and TV crews went about their mysteries.

This was all wasted time.

More of Scott's hours were taken up with eating, sleeping, being a member of a family. This was wasted time too. All Scott wanted was to get back to his Trillions spelling bee and to the problem of making the Trillions understand what writing was *for*.

He found the answer by accident.

During one 'lesson', he had the radio on. He worked so long and late that by the time the lesson was finished, the station had closed down. All that remained on the air was a single whining note. He turned the radio off. The sound annoyed him.

Immediately, the Trillions slowed down. He tried to get them working again, but it was as if they were on strike.

He turned on the radio. The whistling note sounded. The Trillions busily returned to work.

Excited, Scott got out his xylophone – a good toy instrument he had never wished to throw away. He found the note on the xylophone that corresponded to the note sounding from the radio; turned the radio off; and played the xylophone note instead.

The Trillions were happy with it. They went on working, making R's.

Scott bent down and busily destroyed all the R's with his hands. The Trillions were now just so much dust, all over the floor. Then he sounded the xylophone note and kept sounding it. Slowly at first, then faster and faster, the Trillions began to form R's.

His mother appeared in the doorway, half asleep and wearing her nightdress. 'Scott. What *are* you doing? For goodness' sake, it's long after midnight . . .'

'Sorry Mother, I was trying something out.'

'Well, try it out tomorrow! Whatever it is, it can't be so important that—'

'It is important, very important—' Scott blurted out. And immediately wished he had not.

She stood looking at him, uncertainly. His face seemed to her suddenly older, and unfamiliar. What *was* he up to?

'You can't carry the whole world on your shoulders, Scott . . .'

'Of course not, Mother. Good night.'

Had anyone been able to carry the world on their shoulders at this time, he would have found it an uncomfortable burden. Trillions fell and 'formed' their strange, often frightening, shapes: the world got in a temper, partly from fear but mostly from habit. Primitive tribes squatted on the ground, made sacrifices and blamed their gods. Grown-up nations sat round tables, made speeches and blamed each other for all kinds of things having nothing to do with Trillions.

In Harbourtown, still more Trillions fell – a great storm shower of them. And the Major announced over the loud-speakers a major offensive against the Trillions, centered on an Exterminator – a machine that was to destroy the Trillions fed into it. Meanwhile, all Trillion truck teams were to report for duty, immediately. So Scott could not start until evening.

He took his sheets of white paper and scattered Trillions over them. Some of the Trillions shifted and moved without purpose.

He sounded the note that meant R on the xylophone. The Trillions formed R's. Scott scattered them before the letters were formed, then sounded the note again.

'It all depends on whether they *like* work,' he murmured to himself. Once again, the Trillions were forming the letter R. As long as the note sounded, they worked fast and hard. Scott scattered them again. 'R means the note – the note means R. Go on, blast you! R means the note – the note means R.'

There was silence. Scott would not sound the note. The Trillions would not form.

'Go on, go *on* ...!' grated Scott. He sounded the xylophone, then muted the note with his finger. Some Trillions moved, then subsided. It went on like this for an hour, for two hours. Scott found his jaws were aching: he had been clenching his teeth in the effort to force his will on the Trillions – to point a ray from his mind, almost, at the little glittering heaps.

At last they obeyed. Though Scott had sounded the note only in his mind, there was a sudden scurry of movement on one piece of paper. Some Trillions were forming. Scott craned towards them, growling 'Go on, go on, go on! R! R!'

The Trillions formed an R. Scott let out a great shout of 'Whoopee!' Then 'thought' the note harder still.

All the Trillions formed, furiously. There were R's everywhere! Scott tried to reach over his own shoulder to pat himself on the back. He couldn't, and giggled instead. Then he sat down to work out the next steps in the Trillions' education.

'They like work,' he said to himself. 'They want a master – someone to tell them what to do. They've learned. Fine. And now ... what?'

Outside, the Trillion trucks rattled and banged in the streets, the children whooped and hollered.

Scott told his mother that he had something wrong with

his stomach – he felt sick. She looked hard at his face. It was white and there were dark patches under his eyes. 'They won't like it,' she said. 'Your being away from the Trillion Truck, I mean. They're very strict about it. But you do look ill, you really do . . .'

'I feel ill,' Scott said. He did, too. Ill with excitement. Ill with a fever to get back to his room, to his Trillions, to the next step forward.

'Well, I'll see to it,' said his mother. 'Could you eat an omelette, do you think?'

'Oh, yes!' said Scott. 'A big – I mean a bit of one.'

He ate the omelette, drank three glasses of milk, took two apples, a banana and an orange while his mother's back was turned, and made sure that he walked slowly and heavily up the stairs, like someone feeling ill.

Then he closed his bedroom door behind him, took a deep breath and said to the Trillions, 'All right. Back to work!'

Later, he was glad of the fruit. He had not imagined how exhausting it would be – how hard it was to aim his mind as if it was a rifle, to shoot his will at the Trillions like a bullet – and to keep aiming, keep shooting, without ever relaxing, until the Trillions could 'hear' his mind as well as they could hear the note of the xylophone.

By evening, the xylophone had been pushed back under the bed. It was no longer needed: the Trillions had learned to obey the commands 'start', 'stop', 'all', and 'only you'. Scott threw these commands at them with his brain. Now he could make groups of Trillions, or all the Trillions, start to form – or stop forming.

He taught them to use the alphabet. He would think A
– form a picture of the letter in his mind, then beam it at
the Trillions. Then he would think, 'Start A' – 'Stop A' –
'All start A' – 'Only you start A' – and the Trillions would
mesh and climb and gear and build.

'You really don't look well, Scott,' said his mother at
dinner that night. 'I've never seen you look so pale. You'd
better stay home tomorrow. I'll send word to the Trillion
Truck sergeant.'

'All right, mother,' Scott said meekly. To himself, he
said, 'And I'll send words to the Trillions. Not just letters.
Whole words!'

But then, just as the lessons were reaching the most
interesting stage, they had to stop. The General was back:
the General was on the warpath. You could tell when the
General was on the warpath, simply by watching him
march along it. During the past twenty-four hours he
had marched up and down, back and forth, to and fro,
at enormous speed. The Major had almost to trot to keep
up with him. The Lieutenants, non-commissioned officers
and mere private soldiers who always attended the General
– they formed a small private army – scuttled along behind,
looking tough, determined, fearless and baffled.

The townspeople looked baffled too. What were the
army people up to?

Mina found out, simply by asking.

She had long since lost her slight fear of the General. He
was, after all, only a man, and Mina thought of males as
spiders think of flies. Once she had very nearly managed

to sit on his lap, but the General escaped by standing up, rather quickly.

You could just detect an air of caution in the attitude of the General now, as Mina approached. The General and his staff happened to be in the Houghton living-room where some local maps had been left. Mr Houghton and Icarus were there. No one else, of course, could have got near the General for he was ringed round by his staff and busily consulting a map held on a clipboard. Mina broke through the circle simply by piping 'Excuse *me*! Excuse *me*!' in a piercingly sweet voice. She attracted the General's attention equally simply: she took hold of his tunic and pulled.

'Aren't your soldiers working *hard*, Mister General?' she said.

The General pretended only just to have noticed her; saluted; and replied, 'Yes, my dear. So am I. Run along, if you please.'

'And the lights are on all night where they're building the Sterminator, aren't they, Mister General?' she continued brightly.

'Exterminator,' the General corrected her. 'And good day to you.'

'But what's the good of the Sterminator, Mister General?' said Mina.

'Gets rid of Trillions.'

'But more and more Trillions keep coming down, don't they, Mister General?' Mina said.

The General said, 'Quite so, highly observant. Now, if you please—'

Then Mina asked the question that everyone in

Harbourtown West wanted to ask. 'What's the good of it all, then?' she said sweetly.

'What indeed,' said the General. Then he saluted, turned on his heel and marched away. Mina simply turned to the Major and continued her questions. 'Why don't you blow up all the Trillions, Mister Major?' she said. 'I bet you could! With a great big gun!'

The Major knew even less than the General how to deal with the awful sweetness, the sweet awfulness, of this terrible little girl who asked questions. He swelled and said, 'Ha ha ha.' But Mina had fixed him with her big beautiful eyes: he had to say something more.

'No need for great big guns, little girl! TNW, that's the medicine!'

'TNW?' cried Mina, her voice louder and clearer than any bell – 'TNW? I've never heard of TNW! What's TNW?'

The General had stopped in his tracks. He turned to the Major. Everyone saw that the General's leather face had gone an odd colour, as if the leather had been lightly dusted with talcum powder.

'Major!' he almost shouted. 'Here if you please!'

'TNW?' repeated Mina, knowing full well that the cat had been let out of the bag – and she had opened it. 'What a funny name for medicine! Tee . . . Enn . . . Doubleyew!'

Everyone but Mina seemed frozen. The Major looked as if he had been punctured. The General seemed turned to dusty stone. Scott's father was staring fixedly at the General. Icarus Blythe, who had been almost lying in an armchair, was on his feet.

Then everyone was talking and moving at once.

'Can I have some TNW?' said Mina. 'Can we all have some?'

'We can all have some,' Blythe repeated after her. 'Now run along.' He looked very angry indeed.

Mrs Houghton entered the room and said, 'What is all this?'

Bem answered. 'T for Tactical. N for Nuclear. W for weapons. TNW. That's right, isn't it, Icarus?'

'You mean – nuclear weapons, here – here in Harbourtown West . . . ?' asked Mrs Houghton, faintly. 'But that's absurd!'

'Quite absurd,' said Icarus bleakly.

'The Trillions haven't actually *done* anything . . .' Mrs Houghton said. 'They just – just build their silly structures – they don't *mean* anything, do they?'

Icarus shook his head.

'Then why this talk about nuclear weapons? What *for*? What's the good of it? What will happen?'

'Nothing good,' said Mr Houghton, grimly. 'What does happen when you start messing about with these weapons? How will it affect us?'

Icarus, Scott saw, was becoming more than just angry. His movements were jerky and uneasy. His scars were white. His voice was unsteady.

'Nobody knows much about nuclear weapons. Tactical nuclear weapons are small weapons, supposed to have a strictly local effect. A sort of nuclear machine gun, if you like, instead of a nuclear bomb. But poisonous all the same . . . because nuclear weapons don't merely burn, blast and break things. They can alter life forms. They distort and twist, change the way things grow, destroy the patterns of nature. Once you start messing about with nuclear devices—'

'Mr Blythe,' the General cut through, 'we face menace. Or rather, fail to face it. I have yet to observe a statesman, or politician or—' the words came out as an insult – '*man of science* like yourself, offer a positive answer to a definite menace. Wet hens in a thunderstorm. Therefore—'

'Therefore you'll lead us into even worse trouble with nuclear weapons,' said Blythe.

'I shall lead you,' said the General. 'I shall most certainly lead. And you, in your *advisory* capacity, will follow. Be quite clear about that.'

There was a knock on the door and a young Lieutenant entered without waiting for anyone to say 'Come in'. He saluted, yelped 'Sir!' to the General, and said, 'Trouble, sir. They've been forming. In the harbour. Enlarging the fort, sir.'

'Trillions?'

'Yes, sir, Trillions—'

'Then say so.'

The General swept out. 'I think it's about time,' said Mrs Houghton, 'that the General stopped using this house as a sort of unofficial headquarters. At first it was just inconvenient, but now—'

'For that matter, it's about time they stopped using our town as a military HQ for the western world,' said Mr Houghton bitterly.

'Oh, they'll move out of your home,' said Blythe. 'The General has got his soldiers building for him. But leave this town – no, I don't think so. Why? Because Trillions started here. Because Trillions are still happening here. Because Harbourtown is a perfect test area. But above all, because the General is determined to *act* . . . and he can't get the authority.'

'He certainly won't get it from the United Nations,' said Mr Houghton. 'That business on television – nations walking out – hopeless.'

'He won't get it from his own superiors either,' said Blythe. 'They can't make up their minds. So he's forming his own military empire, here in Harbourtown.'

'So we're to be the guinea-pig town,' said Mrs Houghton faintly. 'The General's "test area" . . . The playground for the man of action . . .'

No one could think of anything to say.

There was a mild sun over the harbour, giving the little waves a milky glitter. A great many people crowded the walls. They all looked towards the knot of boats in the widest part of the harbour bowl. The boats bobbed together. In the centre of them was the Harbourmaster's launch, a bigger vessel than the others, which rolled slightly in a dignified way. Standing on its decks were four glistening figures in underwater gear, black rubber with yellow seams. One was reloading an underwater camera.

Scott nodded to Bem and Blythe. Without a word, they got into Mr Houghton's fibreglass dinghy and quietly rowed out to join the knot of boats. As they splashed through the water, they could observe the young Lieutenant going from one group to another on the shore, obviously asking for a boat to take the General out. No one was being very helpful.

When they reached the boats, everything was quiet and they could hear every word that was being said on the launch . . .

'About two hours, probably sooner,' said the skin-diver with the camera. 'Or I could get down there again and take Polaroids. Then you wouldn't have to wait for the films to be processed. Only I've left the Polaroid back for the camera at home—'

'I don't see why you need panic about photographs,' said another skin-diver. 'Just get a mask on and snorkel, and go and see for yourself. It's all there, only a few feet down. Like a toy fortress rising from the seabed. You know, walls and towers – like we said. About seventy feet high and three hundred feet long. All made of Trillions. It's just like a fortress, a toy fort.'

'A toy fortress, you said?' repeated a reporter, looking up from his notepad.

'For heaven's *sake*—' said the skin-diver disgustedly. 'How many more times . . .'

There seemed nothing to say or do for the moment. Some people peered over the edge of their boats, trying to glimpse the tops of the towers. The photographers fiddled with their cameras. The hard blonde reporter, who always seemed to be everywhere, put down a portable tape recorder and picked up a lipstick.

Then the General arrived. The Lieutenant had persuaded someone to lend him a little dinghy. A sweating soldier rowed, another carried the General's valise and a walkie-talkie, the Lieutenant knelt to attention in the bows and the General sat bolt upright in the stern. Heads turned to watch the approaching boatload. The soldier at the oars, unused to his work, was digging at the water: the boat came forward in uncertain spurts and jumps. At each dig of the oars, another gallon or so of water would spill over the gunwhales and into the overloaded boat. The General's magnificent boots were already awash to the ankles. He did not condescend to notice this, though by moving his feet a few inches they would have remained dry.

'Halt!' said the General as his dinghy bumped into the others. Then, 'Radio Operator!' The soldier handed him the walkie-talkie.

'Clear this area!' barked the General. Voices babbled, but the General took no notice. Sure enough, the knot of small boats began to break up and make for the shore.

The General addressed his walkie-talkie. 'TNW section, report!' he ordered. The walkie-talkie squeaked a response.

'But General—' said Icarus.

'You will kindly leave the area,' said the General, staring through him and returning his attention to the walkie-talkie. 'TNW section, prepare to receive your orders!' said the General.

Later, only three craft were visible in the harbour waters, all manned by soldiers. Two of the boats were armed with small, shining tubular weapons, whose barrels were pointed downwards into the water.

In the third craft sat the General, like a figure carved from mahogany.

*   *   *

Icarus, white with fury, either had nothing to say or was too choked with rage to say it. Scott could get nothing out of him. Perhaps it was Panda's large black eyes, staring at him as mournfully as a dog's, that at last made him forget his own rage and think of things that mattered more. He picked up Panda and sat her on his lap and talked over the top of her head to Scott.

'How far have you got with your Trillions?'

'Much farther. I didn't want to tell anyone until I was quite sure, but—'

'Scott, it's either these – these military morons – or us. Either we can do it the right way, your way, or they'll be blasting off their TNWS . . . and to hell with Harbourtown West and everywhere else. Once they've started, there is no telling where it will end—'

He glanced down at Panda and checked himself.

'Scott, you've *got* to succeed. Fast. You've *got* to get in touch with the Trillions – understand them, talk to them, anything you like . . . Is there anything that Bem or I can do to help?'

'I don't think so. It's a job for one person and I'm doing very well. If only I could make things go faster!' Scott got up, scratched his head and stared out over the harbour. The shining tubes of the nuclear guns caught the sun.

'I'm going back home,' said Scott. 'I'm going to try—'

But at that moment, the loudspeakers began to blare. 'EVERYONE IS TO RETURN TO THEIR OWN HOMES AND STAY INDOORS UNTIL FURTHER INSTRUCTIONS. STAY

INDOORS UNTIL FURTHER INSTRUCTIONS. EVERYONE IS
TO RETURN TO THEIR OWN HOMES—'

The loudspeakers were drowned by the roar of military
trucks. The trucks stopped at intervals, soldiers jumped
down and began to shepherd the people away from the
sea wall and back to their homes.

The General still sat bolt upright in his boat and the
little figures of the soldiers were busier than ever over the
glinting guns.

Chapter Six

The explosions, when they came, hardly disturbed Scott. They were not loud. They barely shook the window panes. He turned his head towards the window of his bedroom, half expecting to see smoke arising from the area of water where the nuclear weapons had been fired, but there was no smoke. He stared unseeingly for a little while, then shook his head and returned to what really mattered: his Trillions.

Soon, he knew, they would be able to 'talk'.

The floor of his room was littered with big sheets of paper, each with a single word written on it with a felt-nibbed pen: STOP. START. WORK. SCOTT. TRILLIONS.

The discarded sheets were weighted down with Trillions. A sheet on which was written the word DANCE had attracted a mass of Trillions who had exactly imitated the word. But the sheet that Scott looked at again and again had the word WORK written on it in his handwriting – and on this sheet, the Trillions had written the word START.

Scott thrilled. For he knew now that the Trillions could do more than merely imitate. They could make a reply, express a thought. They could tell him, in words, that they wanted the WORK to START.

The General, too, was happy.

The underwater fortress of Trillions was destroyed – it had crumbled to nothing under the blasting shock of the nuclear blast. All that was left, according to the radarechoes. was a flat surface, a mixture of sand, silt and of course Trillions. Eventually, when any risk of contamination was over, skin-divers could go down and see for themselves. But in the meantime, the radar waves told a story that everyone could believe – even Icarus.

So now Icarus fell from favour in Harbourtown West, and the townspeople began to speak highly of the General. You had to hand it to him – he got things moving! He got action!

People who supported Icarus replied, 'Action against what? A structure that happened to look like a toy fortress – a fort without weapons or soldiers?' But the supporters of the General shrugged, even when the fish killed by the explosion came to the surface of the harbour waters, floated belly-up against the harbour wall and began to rot and stink. And soon, things happened in Harbourtown that made everyone forget the smell of dead fish; things that made it seem all the more likely that the General was right and that the Trillions were deliberate enemies of mankind. For instance . . .

Mr Binding was a very old man who lived in the old people's home. He loved cherries – they reminded him of summer in the country when he was a boy.

One day, a van called at the home and men delivered baskets of shining cherries – a treat for tomorrow. But Mr Binding wanted cherries today.

Quite late that night, Mr Binding put on his slippers, crept down the stairs in the dark, found his way to the larder and – using his nightclothes as a basket – collected a private feast of cherries.

Still in the dark, he ate them all, one by one. As he ate, his old eyes grew round with greed; his old gums crushed the soft flesh of the fruit (you do not need teeth to eat cherries); and his old, brown-mottled hands trembled with pleasure as they took more cherries to his stained mouth.

At last, he had no cherries left. only a lap full of stones. How could he get rid of them?

He gathered the folds of his clothing around the stones and shuffled to the back door of the home. There was only one bolt to undo and the key was in the lock: soon he was out in the garden. Though it was pitch dark, he knew just where he was and what was around him in the blackness – to his right, there were dense bushes. All he had to do was to take handfuls of the cherry stones and throw them away. They would all be lost in the bushes and no one would ever know how clever he had been in stealing the cherries.

He smiled as he dipped his hand into the mass of cherry stones. He chuckled as he cast the first handful away from him towards the bushes some feet away.

But the stones he threw came back at him, as if someone had caught each one and thrown them at him.

Mr Binding's mouth fell open: it was no longer smiling.

He took another handful of cherry stones and threw them into the blackness – threw them harder this time. But they came rattling back, harder than before.

Mr Binding began to whimper.

He peered into the darkness. and saw – nothing. What was there to see? Only bushes. Only darkness.

So he picked up a third handful of cherry stones and flung them with all his might, high into the darkness. There was a moment's pause, and back they came – a shower of cherry stones, that hit the top of his head! One even lodged, damply sticky, in his trembling, outstretched hand.

Mr Binding stamped his feet and made a queer little sound in his throat.

He began to throw away cherry stones furiously, cursing them as he flung them. But always they came back, as if a thousand black, invisible imps were catching them – throwing them back – mocking, taunting, jeering!

Mr Binding made a still queerer noise. He clutched his throat and sank to his knees. His heart was thumping, pumping, jumping. His eyes were staring, but they could see nothing in the darkness.

And in the darkness, he died.

In the morning, they found Mr Binding. The cause of his death seemed obvious: he was a very old man who had overstrained himself.

But then another old gentleman in the home, Mr Bellamy, met a reporter and told him that there was more to Mr Binding's death than cherry-stealing. The reporter bought Mr Bellamy a pint of beer and said, 'Go on, then! Tell me!'

Mr Bellamy, after many crafty nods and throat-clearings and another pint of beer, told the reporter that he had got up very early in the morning, looked out of the window in the dawn light – and seen a *wall* in the garden! A wall right against the line of bushes! A wall that had glittered in the pale early sun – and had later disappeared!

'Trillions?' said the reporter. 'Trillions!' said Mr Bellamy. '*They* built the wall, you see. A wall of Trillions!'

'But Trillions are always "forming" into things,' said the reporter.

'Ah!' said Mr Bellamy, 'that may be. But it's funny, isn't it, that once that wall of Trillions had killed poor old Binding, all the Trillions just seemed to sneak off and disappear! Almost as if they'd done it deliberately, and then wanted to hide what they'd done . . . !'

The reporter wrote this story for a syndicate of local newspapers and thought no more about it. Other, cleverer reporters thought differently. Mr Binding's strange death became a news item in more than one continent. Mr Bellamy appeared in the most important of the never-ending TV programmes about Trillions – a programme seen in America, Britain and other English-speaking countries. To

Harbourtown viewers, it was strange to see the old chap among so many faces, including the General's. But Mr Bellamy told his story with relish. The audience warmed to him. The programme became almost cosy because of him.

Then the interviewer turned to the General. 'What do you make of this sad business of Mr Binding, General?'

The General said nothing for some seconds. In those seconds, the cosiness evaporated and something as startlingly clear and cold as the General's eyes took possession of the studio.

'This business of Mr Binding,' he said, 'is the business that brings us back to basics.'

'Such as?'

'Such as Purpose. Power. Action. What purpose did the Trillions have? What powers have they got? How do we propose to act?'

'Well, your first point – purpose – do you mean that the Trillions deliberately destroyed this old man? What purpose would they have in doing that? I mean, you don't suggest—'

'I don't suggest, but I have an opinion. Everyone here has an opinion and combined opinions lead to the formation of a purpose.'

'Yes, well . . . What is your opinion?'

'Mr Binding's death was of no importance to the Trillions but of the greatest importance to us as a demonstration of their powers.'

'You mean that from the Trillions' point of view, the death was incidental, just a side effect?'

'The side effect of a tactical exercise. Yes. The purpose of the Trillions was to try out another expression of their powers.'

'By killing an old man?'

'By building a particular form of structure so as to observe its effectiveness in a particular situation. Purpose and power – basics.'

'And if the try-out was satisfactory, you think we may see the Trillions doing the same thing again?'

'I really *cannot* think,' interrupted a scientist who had spoken earlier, 'that the good General asks us to believe that the Trillions are about to start a sort of world campaign directed at old men eating *cherries* . . !'

There was some laughter.

'What do you answer to that, General?'

'Mr – er – the gentleman opposite me has already given the answer in his own words.'

'I don't understand you—'

'He began by saying, "I really cannot think". I agree.'

This time there was a full-blooded roar of laughter. The cameras held the General's face. He did not so much as blink. Before the laughter had died down, the General resumed speaking. The audience quietened at once.

'I spoke of three basics,' said the General, 'and I have dealt with only two.'

'Your third was action.'

'Quite so.'

'Well, perhaps you will explain to everyone here just what action—'

'There may be others here who have a course of

action to propose. The gentleman opposite, for example?'

Unwisely, the scientist answered.

'I can only say that in a situation like this – the Trillions situation – when you're dealing with organisms, if that is the word, whose purposes and powers are so completely un-understood – that is, incomprehensible—'

'Yes?' said the General's voice. The word fell like a chunk of ice.

'Well, in our present state of information, to speak of action is to speak of – of – surely we must *evaluate*, we must *understand*, we must form an *appreciation* of the menace of the Trillions . . .'

'Menace?' barked the General. 'Did you say "menace"?'

'Well, *if* they are a menace – I mean, we cannot tell yet—'

'I see,' said the General. And sat back, stone-faced.

There was a bleak silence until the interviewer said, 'Well, General?'

'I beg your pardon?'

'Have you any more to add, General?'

'Only that I agree completely with the gentleman opposite. He said "menace". I say "menace". We are agreed.'

'But your third basic, General – Action—'

'Ah,' said the General. His face filled the screen. 'Action! I know how unpopular that word is today. Both among the leaders and the led. I have listened to countless discussions such as this one and have learned nothing from them that

I did not already know – that we face a mysterious enemy and so forth. A menace . . .'

'We are running short of time, General,' said the interviewer, glancing at his watch.

'We are indeed. The world is running short of time. And I am running short of patience. Patience with men who talk of "understanding" and "evaluating" something we agree to be a menace. Men who would rather talk than act. My background is military; I am by training a man of action—'

'Fascist!' shouted someone in the audience. But a still louder voice answered, 'Throw that moron out!' and the audience was quiet again.

'I tell you that we have the means to take action – to fight a menace of any kind, even coloured dust. We have powers and purposes of our own. And there are men among us who want action. Now. Immediately, I am one of them. I will continue to press for action, effective action, strong action. Such views may be unfashionable, but—'

Voices in the audience cried 'No!' and 'We're with you!'

'—But I stick to them, whatever nonsense I must endure from people in high places who – but enough of that. I say, action. Action of the sort I have already taken. Action with the most powerful and effective weapons at our disposal . . .'

But he could no longer make himself heard. The cheering of the studio audience drowned his voice. Viewers saw, through the credit lines, the interviewer point at his watch, shrug his shoulders, wave an arm to someone offscreen. A man could be seen, indistinctly, as he leapt to the stage and attempted to shake the General's hand. Then it was all over. The announcer's face appeared, apologizing for the fact that the programme had over-run by two and a half minutes.

As the headlines of the world's newspaper showed the next day, no apology had been needed.

At one o'clock that morning, when the rest of the family slept, Scott reached his goal and established the bridge between humankind and the Trillions.

He could write messages in plain English to them. They could reply, in handwriting made of their own 'bodies', to him.

Once established, the process rapidly became easier, quicker and more certain. It was like teaching a little boy to swim. It may take months getting him to enter the water without screaming with fear; weeks to teach him to make a few strokes without choking and panicking; then, quite suddenly, the little boy swims and won't stop swimming.

So it was with the Trillions. Now they could express thoughts in writing, promptly. And Scott, on fire with excitement, began to find out what they were and what they thought.

'*Trillions, where from?*' he thought and wrote.

The Trillions formed into uncertain shapes. Scott bit his lip. He recognized what was happening. They were 'scribbling' – trying to find a right answer, or words in which to put their answer. But at last their reply came.

'*Out there. Sky.*'

'*From a planet?*' Scott wrote.

The Trillions wrote /, which meant Yes. X meant No. ? meant Cannot Reply, or Don't Know. This arrangement saved time.

'*Which planet?*' wrote Scott.

The Trillions promptly replied. '*Home.*'

'*Why leave your planet, why come here?*' wrote Scott.

'*Planet gone,*' the Trillions replied. Then they began writing again. '*Planet die. Explod.*'

Scott knew that 'explod' meant 'explode' – the Trillions often made spelling mistakes – but had to have a better answer, so he asked, '*Why explode?*'

'*?*'

'*Was it a war?*'

'*X*'

'*Is the planet gone or is it dead?*'

'*Dead. Gone. No planet.*'

Scott had a vision of a dying planet, too old and weak to hold itself together: a planet that had, after countless centuries crumbled, split asunder and broken like a snowball. But the Trillions were writing again . . .

'*X hom for us,*' appeared on the sheet of white paper. Scott bit his lips, tried to understand, failed and wrote '???'

The Trillions scribbled, then wrote again.

'*No hoem for us. Find new hoem.*'

Now Scott thought he understood. The Trillions had been flung from their planet when it died and broke up. Because they were almost indestructible, they had not

82

died as humans would die. Instead, they had travelled or drifted through space seeking a new home – and had found Earth. He longed to know if their search had been a lengthy one and if they had visited other planets. But there were more important questions. What did they do on their own planet? What were they intending to do on Earth?

So he wrote, '*What did Trillions do on home planet?*'

'*Build,*' the Trillions replied.

'*Build what?*'

'*As told.*'

Scott felt his excitement rising.

'*Who told you what to build?*'

'*Good masters,*' came the answer.

Scott wrote, '*Masters?*' and the Trillions wrote /.

'*Who were your masters?*'

The Trillions scribbled for a long time, then wrote '*Good at home. Made home good.*'

Scott thought about this. The Trillions found it hard to describe their masters. The best description they could find was, 'good' – a word they had used three times. Probably, then, the Trillions had been simple servants under a 'master' they could not understand but always obeyed faithfully. He decided to try once more for a description of the masters.

'*Your masters like us?*' he wrote, but got only uneasy scribblings in reply. He decided to try a new tack.

'*Where masters now?*'

'*Dead gone with planet.*'

'*Who tells you what to do now masters gone?*'

There was a great deal of scribbling, then the answer came. *'Build like masters home planet.'*

Perhaps, thought Scott, they meant that as they always built on their home planet, they must build still – it is the only thing they know, the only usefulness they have. He tested this idea by writing, *'Why build?'*

'Like home planet.'

Ah, Scott said to himself, I was right. The Trillions were like honeybees – working from habit, working skilfully without reason, working for the sake of the work in obedience to a force they did not need to understand. But, no: this was not good enough. The Trillions were showing intelligence. They were answering his questions. They had learned to write. They were more than blind slaves. They had to have a reason for what they did – a purpose in their visit to Earth.

He wrote, *'Who are your masters now?'*

The Trillions scribbled, began to form a word, scribbled again. At last they wrote, *'Good planet.'*

'Am I your master?' Scott wrote.

The Trillions formed a /, then an X, then repeated what they had written before – *'Good planet.'*

Scott wrote, *'This planet?'* and the Trillions merely answered with the Yes sign.

Scott sighed. He was more or less back where he had started with the 'honeybee' theory – the idea of the blindly obedient workers. His head ached and his eyes itched with tiredness. He decided to write only two more questions before sleep overtook him.

'What will you do for this planet?'

'*Build*' came the answer. Scott smiled to himself. It was what he had expected.

'*What can we do for you?*' he wrote.

The answer came back as quickly, violently and directly as a blow in the face.

'*Hate us.*'

Before he fell into a nightmare sleep, Scott tried everything to change the Trillions' answer. Had they meant 'Heat', not 'Hate'? Their answer came back – X. He put the question into different words, but it made no difference.

At last, he fell asleep knowing that there could be no mistake. Hate us, hate us, *hate us* . . . In the dark, he seemed to see the glittering Trillions form the word. In his sleep, he dreamed of the General's face looming from the television screen, shouting 'FOE!'

When he woke next morning his eyes ached and his head was agony. He swung his feet out of bed. His legs felt heavy. The floor of his room was a litter of paper, scrawled with his own writing. The daylight streamed in; perhaps what had happened a few hours earlier had been part of a long nightmare? But there on the floor was the same piece of paper bearing the same message.

'*Hate us.*'

He lifted the paper by two corners and flung the Trillions from him, then went to the bathroom to wash. Outside, the usual morning din had already started as the Trillion Trucks and their crews prepared for action. They could do without him today, Scott thought.

Back in his room, he saw the Trillions forming on their sheet of paper. He watched with fascination and disgust to see what they would write.

The words were '*Good home. Work.*'

Chapter Seven

'Plan A,' said the General.

There was a jumbled mumbling of interpreters. A Russian General said 'Da, da, da' impatiently and a German General was having trouble with his earphones. A photographer took a flash photograph and a uniformed man ran up and hissed and flapped at him. The photographer made loud protests, in French. The blonde woman journalist smiled a painted smile, took a tiny miniature camera from her suede jacket and photographed the incident.

'Plan A,' said the General, loudly and firmly. Slowly, the meeting came to order.

'Plan A,' said the General. 'For discussion and I hope approval by all parties present. Representing seventeen nations. Right.'

The Russian General scowled, said 'Da, da, da' again

and deliberately broke the lead of his pencil on the clean white pad in front of him.

'First,' continued the General, 'We must establish nature of foe. Know what he is, what he's doing, what he might do.'

This caused the interpreters some trouble to translate. The Russian General shifted his earphones so that only one ear was covered, then took out a penknife and began to sharpen his pencil. The chips of wood flew in all directions. The Chinese General near him made the chips into a little pile.

'Establish nature of foe,' said the General. 'To do this, we will consider implications of film showing Trillions' activities here and abroad. Show film!' A soldier called 'Lights!' Another soldier brushed his hand over switches. Now the big room was almost dark.

It was a dull room – merely a great featureless concrete-coloured hall. The Army had erected it from prefabricated units only two days earlier. But the people in the room were colourful enough. Round the central square of tables sat men of many nations, most of them in military uniform and all of senior rank. There were white, pink, brown, yellow and black skins: blue, brown, buff, grey and white uniforms. The General's soldiers, who acted as attendants, wore white-painted steel helmets, brilliant white belts, webbings and holsters, white anklets and white gloves on their tan uniforms. Not one soldier was less than six feet tall. Their boots shone as if treacle had been poured over them. The splendour of the military men made the civilians look dull and ordinary. Icarus, who had folded himself into an untidy lump on an uncomfortable wooden chair, was lost in the crowd.

The room darkened until only the soldiers' white webbing stood out. The film began. An American Army Officer commented into his hand microphone: the translators murmured into theirs.

'Harbourtown West,' said the American Army Officer, keeping his voice flat and dry. 'First reports of Trillions. Date, 11 June.' The screen showed the scene – the drifts of Trillions in gutters, a close-up of Trillions, a darker patch in a sunny sky containing more Trillions about to fall.

'Da, da, da' said the Russian General, disgustedly.

But even he sat up a little later when the screen showed the underwater Trillion 'fortress'. And there was complete silence, complete attention, for the film sequences taken during the last few days.

'Paris, France,' announced the American Officer. The screen showed a street crowded with people, all with their heads turned to the dark sky. The cars in the street had stopped. It was raining Trillions. The camera showed a close-up of Trillions bouncing off the shoulders of a man's overcoat. The man constantly brushed at the Trillions in his hair with one hand. The camera pulled back into long focus. Everyone seemed to be brushing themselves while still staring at the sky.

'The heaviest fall of Trillions in Europe,' said the Officer. 'Millions of tons. Now London, England.'

The camera showed the river Thames with Big Ben and the Houses of Parliament in the background. The surface of the water was pocked with the rain of Trillions. A close-up showed the windscreen of a car, wipers going. Trillions formed a thick layer in the angle of screen and body. The camera moved right in on the windscreen and showed a curved pattern of scratches on the glass. The wipers had picked up Trillions: the Trillions had scratched the glass.

'Trillions are almost as hard as diamonds,' said the Officer and added a short description of their physical properties.

'Berlin . . . Amsterdam . . . Hong Kong . . . Moscow . . . Cape Town . . .' There were brief shots of each city. In each, Trillions were falling.

'It is not possible to calculate exactly the total tonnage of Trillions that has descended on this planet,' said the Officer. 'But one authority estimated that sufficient Trillions have fallen to cover the world's land surfaces to a depth of more than one millimetre. This is only an estimation, and not—'

On the table by the Officer, a telephone rang. The Officer picked up the receiver and listened.

'Trillions are at present falling on . . . the south coast of France . . . eastern frontiers of Turkey . . . what was that, Carlsbad? . . . yes, Carlsbad . . . Zürich . . . Black Forest . . . Davos . . . There seems to be a general central-European fall at the moment.' He replaced the receiver.

People were beginning to lose interest. The Chinese General tipped his pile of pencil sharpenings on to the Russian General's pad. The Russian General growled ferociously. The Chinese General smiled and nodded his head as if to say, 'One good turn deserves another.' A

British General grumbled, 'We *know* all this stuff, we *know* it all—' But the dry voice of the American Officer said, 'The forming of Trillions,' and there was complete attention again.

'Trillions forming. Quite a lot of this material is new – some of it only hours old. Much of it has only just been processed. First, Harbourtown West. Underwater. The so-called fortress.'

'We *know* this stuff,' began the British General, but suddenly kept quiet.

'Similar "fortress" in the Black Sea. New material, received this morning,' said the Officer. 'You will notice that this underwater formation is on a very much larger scale. The area covered is some eleven square miles. Maximum depth, 340 feet.'

The cameraman had swung his lens over a great stretch of water. Breaking the surface of the sea, there arose nightmare towers and great haunted turrets, glittering horribly where the light struck them, but dark and secret in the 'windows' and openings.

'These tower-like constructions,' said the Officer flatly, 'rise as high as 200 feet above water. Now, some underwater views of the same constructions.'

Below the water, the Trillion castles seemed even more sinister. The constructions had no meaning – or every meaning. They followed no pattern, suggested no purpose – yet gave an overpowering impression of menace. In every cavern, you could imagine a lurking monster; in every 'window', a grinning devilish face. The Trillions had somehow built palaces of doom and evil.

The screen went white. The telephone rang again. 'Understood,' said the Officer, answering it. He put down the receiver and addressed his audience. 'Film break. The operator is about to splice in important new material. We will continue in about three minutes. Thank you.'

But he was hardly heard. The big hall was buzzing with conversations. Only the General and his soldiers kept quite still and stared straight ahead, expressionless.

From the start, the conference was a world affair. It made headlines in every newspaper throughout the world. Thousands of journalists had tried hundreds of ways to get into the conference hall. Only a few had succeeded.

But Scott was there. And owed it all to Mina.

Her pet soldier, Billy, had been put in charge of the urns supplying the gallons of coffee drunk each day by people attending the conference. It was not a very soldierly or responsible job and Billy had done his best to make it sound more important than it was. Mina pretended to believe him. 'They can't do without you, can they, Billy?' she said, making her eyes big and round.

'You bet they can't, Miss Mina.'

'Not even the General?'

'He's got to have his coffee too. Me and the General,' said Billy, 'are just like *that*!' He clamped two fingers together, and smirked. He felt big. Mina always had this effect on him and she knew it. She also knew that she could be one of the very few people in the whole of Harbourtown West to get into the conference. She did not know what a conference was, or what it was about. But she was determined to go all the same.

She soon found out how to do it. Each morning, a truck delivered groceries including cartons of coffee to the conference. Billy helped unload the truck. He took his cartons of coffee to his little kitchen. One of the cartons said, 'Hello, Billy! Look – I'm wearing my Trillions bracelet. Specially for *you*!'

He pulled open the carton and there was Mina.

When Billy had stopped saying 'But! – but! – but!—' and was able to speak properly, he begged Mina to go. She would not. 'If anyone comes in,' she explained, 'I'll just hide in my carton.'

'But the General . . !' implored Billy. 'If the General finds out!—'

'You and the General are just like *that*,' said Mina primly, making the same sign that Billy had made the day before. 'Can I have a cup of coffee, please? Lots and lots and lots of sugar.'

Mina found coffee-making quite amusing to begin with, but she soon grew tired of filling cups and teasing Billy. She was quite glad when, in the late afternoon, she was packed into her carton and driven away from the conference, and she was delighted when, that evening, she met Bem and Scott. They were talking about the conference. Scott was saying, 'I can't see what conclusion they can reach – I mean, I can't see what good they can do. It isn't just a question of blowing up Trillions—'

'I know,' said Mina, grandly.

The boys ignored her. 'Look at the facts,' said Bem. 'More and more Trillions falling all the time—'

'I know,' said Mina.

'Kick her,' said Bem. 'You're nearest.' Scott did not even look at her.

'Look,' he continued, 'the conference is all military. Nearly everyone there is military—'

'I know,' said Mina. 'I was there all day. Ho, hum, the military. They talk and talk and talk.'

Even she was pleased and surprised by Scott's reaction. His face went white. He seized her by the arm. 'What do you mean, you were there?' he said, in a choked-up voice.

Later, it was all arranged. Scott smuggled himself into the conference just as Mina had done. Mina bullied Billy into showing Scott where to hide himself – it was in the second projection booth, used only for film storage. He had a good view from the little square projection window and safe hiding places behind the storage racks. In exchange, he had only to give Mina any really big ruby-red Trillions he found (she was about to make herself yet another and grander bracelet) and let her off her Trillion Truck duties for a week.

Thus it was that Scott saw and heard everything that happened during the conference. 'We will continue in about three minutes,' the Officer had said. And now the new film material he had promised was spliced together – Scott could hear the soldier in charge of the projector moving about in the next room – and the lights were being dimmed in the big hall.

'This material comes from – Moscow,' said the Officer, keeping his voice flat and cold. 'It is described as being of the greatest possible importance because it shows a new phase in the development of Trillions.'

The screen lit up. Russian characters appeared. Scott could not understand them. Then there were moving pictures of enormous weapons – great rockets on multi-wheeled trailers. Although Scott was a considerable distance away, he could see the Russian General's back straighten and his neck become rigid. Obviously he did not like the pictures on the screen to be shown to an international audience.

The screen went blank for a second and more shots of the weapons appeared. They were taken in a vast concrete launching site. The rockets, now in cradles instead of on trailers, pointed almost straight up into the sky. There were many of them, perhaps twenty or thirty; great steel objects, with numbers painted on their flanks.

Among the audience, heads were turning, people were whispering to each other. The Russian General's head was rigidly upright as if with disgust. The translators' voices were sounding over the loudspeakers in the hall. Too many were speaking at once, but Scott was able to pick out an English-speaking voice saying, 'This is highly confidential material and you are asked not to—'

But then the screen showed a slow panning shot. The camera operator had swung away from the rockets and was covering a wide sweep of bleak countryside, only occasionally broken by leafy birch trees. The lens travelled on until it revealed in the distance a rocket site precisely similar to the first. Against the sky, you could see the same pattern of rockets. The camera moved in on these, closer and closer, until the finned base of a rocket filled the screen. The audience was silent. Closer went the cameras until only the bottom of one fin was shown. This shot was held, then brought into still closer focus to show a glittery, glassy texture.

It was then that Scott and everyone else realized what they were looking at: the 'rocket' was made of Trillions! And the imitation was perfect.

Now the camera was exploring the surfaces of more Trillion 'rockets', but no one watched. The hall was loud with voices. Heads bobbed, hands gestured, men left their chairs and dashed across the floor to speak to colleagues.

Scott saw the General stand on his chair and nod to an Officer who shouted an order. The white-helmeted soldiers guarding each door brought their rifles to the ready. The woman journalist had been making for an exit. A soldier barred her way, with his rifle. She said something, angrily, and the soldier made a small, hard thrusting motion with the rifle. She walked slowly back to her place, looking astonished. Then the General walked briskly to the platform and took a microphone. His amplified voice cut through the babble like a blade through undergrowth.

'MEETING WILL COME TO ORDER. RESUME SEATS. TO ORDER. IMMEDIATELY.'

At once, there was silence and people sat down. Scott felt an unwilling admiration for the upright, leathery little man. The General waited, not bothering even to turn his head, until he had complete attention. Then he said, quietly, 'If you please. Resume business in hand. No further delays. All grateful to Russian friends for releasing most important information. All seen film, understand what we have seen. To business, then. Action.'

He left the platform, marched to his seat at the table, adjusted the microphone in front of him and barked two words into it.

'Plan A.'

He spoke in the tone of one who does not expect to be contradicted and he was not. The new evidence was too strong. At last the nations put their heads together, nodded agreement and decided to act.

The world was prepared for Plan A. Every nation that owned tactical nuclear weapons was instructed to use them. The General was appointed overlord of the operation. It was his voice, and his voice alone, that could give the order to fire. When he spoke, the Trillions would be attacked by explosive powers that made the great bombs of the world war seem like fireworks: by heat so intense that it could turn metal to liquid in a split second.

In Harbourtown West, the loudspeakers had announced that every last Trillion was to be found, collected, delivered and dumped by sundown – General's orders.

'It's mad,' gasped Scott. 'All mad. They've gone mad.'

He gasped because he was running. He was running because he was rushing his Trillion Truck on yet another journey to the Exterminator. The Trillion Trucks were suddenly no longer a joke. Since the conference, everything had changed. At first, the coming of the soldiers had been an annoyance, an excitement, a trial, a scandal – anything you cared to make of it, but nothing really serious. But now, the soldiers were suddenly real and menacing. They were iron men in steel helmets and their guns might fire bullets that actually killed. They had to be obeyed, and obeyed at the double. That was why Scott was running.

Scott, Mina, Panda and Bem reached the Trillion Exterminator plant. They were panting. Ahead of them was a short queue of children and trucks, waiting their turn to tip the Trillions they had collected over the chute. Soldiers holding guns kept the queue moving. The soldiers no longer smiled and joked with the children. They muttered, 'Move along, keep it moving, move along,' and the children sullenly obeyed.

'Where's Billy, mister soldier?' Mina asked the soldier she recognized.

'Move along, keep it moving,' replied the soldier.

'But I want to *talk* to Billy . . .'

'Move along, close up. You lot at the back, get into line.'

The soldier did not even look at her. Yesterday, he had given her a piece of chocolate. Mina's lower lip stuck out and trembled a little.

They tipped out their Trillions, turned the truck round, and started to walk back to collect the next load.

'Double!' said the soldier. 'At the double!'

The teams broke into a jogtrot. Mina ran too, half crying.

When they were nearly back to their area, the fat Major's car swept by and stopped sharply. The driver leapt out, ran to open the door and saluted as the Major got out. As if he were a hunting dog, the Major pointed his sharp nose at the gutter, appeared to sniff, then stood erect.

'You!' he barked, glaring at the children. 'Which one in charge?' His voice was a passable imitation of the General's.

'I am,' said Scott.

'Over here,' said the Major. Scott walked over to him.

'At the double,' growled the soldier who drove the car.

Scott felt his face go hot. He ran to the Major.

'Trillions, lad,' said the Major, pointing at the gutter. 'There. There. And there. Trillions. Sweep up, put in truck, dispose of. NOW.'

'But this isn't even our area,' said Panda.

'At the double,' growled the driver soldier.

Scarlet-faced, the children bent down to pick up the Trillions. There were so few of them that they had to pick them up one by one with their fingers.

'Mad,' said Scott, dully. He was tired and aching.

Bem said, 'I suppose—' then shut up.

'What do you suppose?'

'I suppose they feel they must do something. Anything.'

'But nuclear weapons . . . ! Against Trillions!'

'But you yourself said the Trillions were building rockets in Russia. All kinds of warlike things, all over the world. You said that yourself.' Bem took another bite of his lunch-time sandwich and chewed slowly and miserably. 'All the same, it does seem a bit much. Nuclear weapons, I mean, no one really knows what happens *after*.'

'They just make a lot of noise and burn everything up, don't they?' asked Panda, big-eyed and anxious. 'Nothing happened after they blew up the fortress in the harbour, did it?'

'Did it?' repeated Mina. She was miserable and anxious.

'Oh, *you* . . .' said Bem, looking scornfully at Mina. 'What do you know?'

'That soldier was rude,' said Mina. 'I know that.' She began to cry.

Scott put an arm round her and looked angrily at Bem over her head. Bem looked ashamed. He said, 'Mina is right. Sorry, Mina. The soldier was rude and that's really just what we are talking about. It's all got so—'

'—Serious,' said Panda. 'There's a horrible feeling . . . something bad about to happen, something really bad. I don't know . . .'

'Fallout,' said Bem. 'When you let off nuclear weapons, you can get nuclear fallout. The air is poisoned, plants grow all wrong, people get sick—'

Mina looked up, wide-eyed and afraid.

'Not you, you old silly!' said Panda brightly. 'You'll be all right!' And now it was her turn to glare at Bem.

'The Trillions never really did anything to us,' said Panda. 'Those Russian rockets – it isn't as if the Trillions rockets had anything inside them. They can't fly, they can't do anything, they can't blow up . . .'

They ate in silence. Scott made himself eat too. But drumming in his head were the words 'Hate us . . . Hate us . . . Hate us.'

Chapter Eight

When at last they finished pushing the Trillion Trucks and could go home, the television set showed and talked nothing but Trillions, Trillions, Trillions. Scott switched the dial from one channel to another but it was always the same.

'In this grave crisis of human affairs, the evidence pours in of a world against a common threat—'

He tried another channel.

'—if the existing underwater Trillions barrier were to be extended in this region, the Gulf Stream itself could be diverted and our whole climate changed—'

Try again.

'—scientific age, the ordinary foot-soldier still remains the most sensitive precision weapon we can bring to bear. Only to human hands can we entrust the terrifying power soon to be unleashed against the alien force that—'

He was about to try yet again when Blythe came in.

Scott had almost forgotten about Icarus, yet he had been with him only yesterday evening. He had told Icarus all about his experiments with the talking Trillions: he had told and showed him everything, saving the message 'Hate us!' until last. Icarus had seemed uninterested and distant. 'Nobody else knows about this.' Scott said, trying to underline what he had been saying. Icarus had answered, 'Good thing. Don't tell anyone else. Oh yes, congratulations. It's amazing what you've done . . .'

He had gone, leaving Scott with a picture of a man who was burnt out, useless and defeated. Scott had had no time to worry about this picture. Now, he could hardly believe it had ever existed. For Icarus seemed to be alight, burning, vibrating with urgency.

'Your room,' said Icarus. 'Finish your soup up there. I'll carry this plate. Come on.'

He ran up the stairs to Scott's bedroom with a plate in one hand and a glass of milk in the other. Scott followed, pushed the door shut with his foot and said, 'What's happened? What—?'

'You know what Plan A is, don't you, Scott?'

'Of course. International drive to destroy Trillions with tactical nuclear weapons – burn them to nothing. But—'

'Now listen, Scott. It is my opinion that Plan A will do very little to the Trillions – I think they are more or less indestructible. No, don't interrupt me with questions. I and my research team have done a lot of work in the past days. We've tried everything we know to break them, burn them, explode them – Scott, it's incredible the temperatures they can withstand. You can't touch them chemically, of course. And even when you do break them down physically, I have the feeling that they can eventually form again, even below molecular stage . . . But never mind, I'm wasting time . . .

'As I was saying, I think Plan A can do very little to the Trillions. But I am appalled – appalled and terrified, Scott – at the thought of what Plan A can do to *us*. Look at it this way. No one can say definitely what will happen to us – to Earth itself – when the nuclear blasts begin. There are many people – and I am one of them – who see almost every new thing mankind does as a threat. Pesticides, the dust in space left by atomic explosions, chemical waste from factories—'

'I know all this, I know the argument, we're fouling our planet,' began Scott. But Icarus hurried on.

'And now Plan A. Nuclear weapons all over the planet, all to be fired at the same time Scott, anything can happen—'

'I know, I know. How do we stop it?'

'Ah, how do we stop it. The men who have the power are the Plan A men – the General. Plan A is his toy, his creed and gospel—'

'How do we stop it?'

'Scott, you told me what the Trillions' message was. They said, "Hate us". Just that, "Hate us". When you told me that, I went – sick. I knew, certainly, that nothing could be done. I knew that nothing good could happen – only Plan A. Plan A is as evil as the Trillions: the Trillions are as evil as Plan A. So let the General get on with it, I thought. Either he or the Trillions will finish us all off!'

Watching Icarus, Scott felt infected by his explosive energy. The man was almost raving at him.

'Then something happened, Scott. I was thinking – quite uselessly – about what might happen to us when the nuclear weapons went off. I was thinking of the possible effects on our ecology—?'

'Ecology – the balance of nature,' said Scott. 'The way any one planet or animal or organism depends on another. Yes, I know what the word means.'

'Good. Well, I was thinking how Plan A might be the last straw for this poor old planet of ours . . . Then I thought of the message, "hate us". What does that mean to you?'

'It's a threat,' said Scott, carefully. 'It's a warning. It means, "Right – we are going to hurt you. So the only thing left for people on Earth to do is – hate us"!'

'Have the Trillions ever hurt us, Scott?'

'No. Not hurt. Just . . . make themselves look tough. You know, the Russian rockets and the fortress. Things like that.'

'And what did they do in their previous existence – on their own home planet?'

'They built.'

'What did they build?'

'What their masters told them.'

'So the Trillions could be *ecological organizations*, Scott.'

'Ecological—'

'Look. Imagine a planet. Alive, but not like our planet.

Not with humans on it – not little units walking about that have their own wills, their own inventiveness, their own ideas of progress. Just a planet. But a planet cannot for ever just roll through space. Things change, things happen. So *jobs need doing, all the time*. Now do you begin to understand?'

'No.'

'But it's simple. The side of a mountain collapses, say. A river is diverted. Things – organisms, plants, even animals – that had lived through the river will die. The water they must have to exist is gone. But then the *servants of the planet* are summoned. They form a dam, or new banks, or repair the mountain – they do whatever is needed to restore the river and make things right again.'

'Bees . . . beavers . . .' said Scott softly.

'Yes – but with a difference. Bees work for the good of the hive, beavers for themselves or their little clan. But Trillions – I believe that Trillions worked for the sake of their whole planet – their whole ecology. I believe their planet somehow told them what to do. Or perhaps it was just one particular life from on the planet that was their "master". It doesn't matter what.'

'They said "good planet",' Scott murmured. 'That could mean a planet where their masters always had work for them to do. So they built on each other and made whatever the planet needed . . .'

Pictures of an alien planet formed in his mind. Fantastic vegetation by a river – the crumbling of a mountain of strangely coloured rock – the Trillions answering their master, the planet itself, and building, forming, repairing . . .

'All right – I agree to your theory!' he said. 'It's wonderful, marvellous, terrific. But what's the good of it? What difference does it make if you're wrong or right? What difference does it make to Plan A and the General and the big bang? They don't want to serve *us*, that's all that matters! They've *told* us so! They told me that they hate us!'

'No, they didn't Scott. They never wrote that,' said Icarus. 'They didn't say *they* hated *us*. They said—'

'They said we should hate *them*,' said Scott; and stopped, baffled.

He could almost feel the answer to the riddle of the Trillions burrowing into his mind. And yet—

'Think, Scott,' said Icarus. 'Suppose my theory is right – then think. I'll go through it again.'

He ticked off his argument point by point on his fingers. 'The Trillions exist only to serve their planet, their master. They lose their planet and become like homeless dogs. They find another planet and wish to do the only thing they know – serve, through building. All right so far?'

Scott nodded.

'Then you manage to get through to them; they "serve" you by learning to write your language. Then comes the important moment. You ask the Trillions what we can do for them – and they answer, "Hate us". Now do you see, Scott?'

'No,' said Scott miserably.

Icarus looked at his watch and jumped to his feet.

'Come downstairs with me, Scott!' he said. 'We'll watch the TV news. Then you'll understand!'

Scott watched but could not concentrate. The room was crowded. His parents were there, and two neighbours. Nothing on the screen seemed to touch on what was in his mind, although most of it was about Trillions. There were pictures of weapon carriers, soldiers, mobilizations in various countries, air-strike missiles. There was a brief shot of the General saying 'No comment' to a group of reporters outside a huge, glassy building. Then brief glimpses of Trillion exterminators in action.

He felt a nudge on his elbow. 'What is it all about, Scott?' said Icarus nodding at the screen.

'Thumping the Trillions, I suppose,' said Scott, with a half smile.

'Fine,' said Icarus. 'Keep watching.'

The news droned on. Student trouble in Tokyo. Police with shields and helmets, bursts of flame from petrol bombs. A man in handcuffs being pushed by the police through a crowd of screeching women, then a shot of the house where the murder had been committed. A girl in a bathing suit holding a huge cup. Troops on the border of somewhere or other. A protest march against something or other. A tennis player making the winning smash, a boxer delivering a knockout. Scott could not concentrate. The riddle of the Trillions was still boring at his mind.

Then came a sequence showing a racing car. 'Grand Prix!' said Scott to himself, suddenly waking up. More cars! a whole bunch sweeping into the grandstand corner! Scott peered at the screen, trying to find his favourite driver's car. But then another TV camera picked up a single car and the chance was lost. The camera followed the car into a bend. It was catching a tail-ender. The two cars touched, there was a scream of tyres, a mixed-up, lurching, sliding tangle, then a cloud of smoke with bits of metal bursting from it—

Scott jerked to his feet, eyes wide and staring at Icarus.

'You're right!' gasped Scott. 'It must be that! You're right!'

'How else *could* the Trillions serve us?' demanded Icarus.

'I was a fool not to have seen it,' said Scott. 'I mean, we do everything else so well. We can build – anything, anything at all. What could they do for us?'

'So the Trillions couldn't compete. They came to Earth and found what they needed – a planet on which things were *built*. The Moon wouldn't have been any good – it's dead, so nothing needs to be done. It's possible that they tried a hundred planets – a thousand, a million – before they found us. But we seemed right for them, so down they came—'

'And straight away, they did their tricks, their only trick,' interrupted Scott. 'Just like that lost dog you talked about. They sort of wagged their tails to show willing. They "formed". All we had to do was to say, "Yes, good boy, I understand – you're builders, we can set you to work straight away. You can build for us just as you used to build on your own planet. You can form into dams and breakwaters and landing strips—"'

'But we thought only of destroying them. And just as bad – anything they can do, we can do just as well or probably better. Their rockets were only pointed shapes.

108

Their fortress was only a sham. Even Mina's bracelet is only Trillions, not precious stones. You can't say to Trillions, "Form into a reliable wrist-watch!" or "Be a bath sponge!" They could look like it, but not be it. On their home planet, they were part of the life of the place – and part of the soul, too. But here – well, humans are too clever. They had to find a job, a task, a reason for being allowed to continue to live here.'

'"Hate us",' said Scott. 'That's a rotten job, just being hated.'

'Yes, but what else is there for them? That TV news – for heaven's sake, Scott, what else can they do at this very moment? What would you think if you were the Trillions' collective brain or consciousness or whatever it is they have? It's all a fight, Scott – one long battle. Students against police, army against army, nation against nation, boxer hitting another boxer—'

'There was a girl in a bathing costume.'

'And why was she on the news? Because she had won a fight, a beauty contest.'

'Punching bag,' said Scott thoughtfully. 'That's how the Trillions see themselves. As the punching bag for all our fighting instincts. They know that we never stop fighting. They know that we get better and better all the time at doing each other damage. They must sense that the end is near for this planet – unless we can be switched over to hitting something that doesn't matter and can't be hurt. Though I don't see how that can stop people murdering each other, or crashing racing cars, or having riots in the streets.'

'It can't,' said Icarus. 'But don't you see, that's not the part that matters. That's more or less personal stuff. It's the mass fights that can destroy Earth; the big weapons, the big bangs.'

'The General!' exclaimed Scott. 'We've forgotten about him! You talk of the Big Bangs – he's just getting one ready!'

They went to the window. The Army vehicles were rumbling by, making so much noise that they could no longer talk. There were ordinary trucks, filled with soldiers: tanks, with great guns of a strange pattern: little guns on fat rubber tyres, stranger still: control consoles, again on fat tyres, that presumably were used to direct and fire the nuclear guns: electric generators: things like astronomical aerials – great dished fans made of metallic mesh: and, just occasionally, a human soldier.

'Aliens!' shouted Scott, pointing to the last vehicles in the procession. 'There's your aliens! Mine, anyhow . . .'

'Friend or foe?' answered Icarus, grimly. '*I* don't know which. Could be that we're our own enemy. But that's the whole point, isn't it? Who are the Goodies, who the Baddies?'

Scott rubbed his temples with his fists and said,

'Wait, wait a moment. Where are we? On the one hand, we've got you and me, Bem, Panda, Mina, my parents – oh, nearly everyone we've ever met . . . If you like, the Good People. But then, when you turn on the news, all you seem to see is the work of the Bad People. Killers, vandals, rioters, people hurting and getting hurt . . .'

'Then there's the General.'

'Yes, the General. Is he good or bad? Has he ever done a cruel thing in his life – I mean, has he himself actually used a gun to kill someone? Yet with Plan A—'

'With Plan A, he could condemn half a world to a horrible death for all we know. Good People, Bad People – where do you draw the line? Is that silly soldier of Mina's – you know, Billy – one of the Good people?'

'Of course he is. Old silly Billy.'

'And then the General puts a gun in his hands and gives the order to fire . . . And Billy fires, and a man drops dead and Billy gets a medal?'

'All right, leave it at that. I agree. The Good and the Bad People, they're hopelessly mixed up. They can never be sorted out. Agreed. Then along come the Trillions and we both get excited and talk about punching bags – a target for all our bad instincts—'

'Yes, that's it exactly. A *safe* target.'

'But haven't you forgotten something, Icarus?'

'What?'

'Don't you remember telling me about the time you were alone in space – really alone, you said? Don't you remember saying that space was *alien*?'

'Yes, of course I remember.'

'And I asked you, "Alien good, or alien bad?" And you said something like it being impossible to tell, alien meant alien – completely strange, completely mysterious?'

'So—'

'Alien. Alien, *like the Trillions*. That's what you said.'

'Well, I may have said something like that, yes. What are you driving at?'

'This: you have been talking about the Trillions as if they were old friends of ours – jolly dogs wagging their tails and so on. Wanting to make friends and do their tricks for us. Wanting to serve us. Right?'

'I don't see—'

'Yet you also said that the Trillions were aliens. Which do you mean? Are Trillions dogs wagging their tails – or are they strange, alien beings from space – dangerous foreigners? Because that was the feeling they once gave you.'

'I don't remember saying—' Icarus began, then stopped, staring at Scott. At last he said, 'What are you getting at?'

'We can't tell the difference between the Good People and the Bad People even when we know them – even when they are humans. Billy the soldier can be good one minute, bad the next. We *agreed* that. Yet you seem perfectly willing – so was I at first, I'm not being rude – to say, "Hurrah for Trillions! Trillions must be good, because they told us so!" Yet not so long ago, they were giving you another dose of the most frightening feeling you've ever had—'

'Aliens . . .' breathed Icarus. 'You're right, of course, Scott. What a fool! They're aliens. And for all I know, the best liars in the whole universe . . .'

Icarus got to his feet and began walking back and forth. Scott watched him, miserably. 'The sickening thing about it,' he said, 'is that you might have been right – I mean, perhaps the Trillions really are the Good People, they really do mean to act as targets or punchbags—'

'No. It won't wash. We have to be sure.'

'We never can be sure,' reasoned Scott. 'How do you find out? Go and visit a planet that no longer exists – having first become a Trillion, of course?'

There was silence, then Icarus said, 'Yes.'

'Yes, what?'

'Yes – do what you said! Go and visit that planet that doesn't exist! Become a Trillion!'

'For heaven's sake! – You're joking!—'

'Do I look as if I'm joking, Scott? Do I? Can't you see what I'm getting at? Don't you remember how you taught the Trillions in the first place – by drilling into them with that extraordinary mind of yours?

'Well, Scott – drill deeper! Drill right inside them! Take your mind clean through them and out the other side! Dig into their memory, their history, their past!'

When Scott spoke, his voice trembled. 'What a mad idea!' he said. 'What a terrific idea!'

'Will you *try* it?'

'Of course. Tonight!'

Alone in his room, Scott clenched his jaws, focused his mind and shot it at the Trillions. TELL ME. SHOW ME. TAKE ME BACK WITH YOU. LET ME REMEMBER YOUR MEMORIES . . .

Some Trillions grouped: Scott's heart leaped. They began to write. He craned forward to watch.

'*?*' the Trillions wrote.

Scott cursed and began again. Again. Again. Despairing, he even wrote his questions down on big sheets of paper as well as beaming them with his mind.

TELL ME ABOUT HOME PLANET. TELL ME ABOUT GOOD MASTERS.

GOOD PLANET, the Trillions replied.

TELL ME WHAT WORK YOU DID. WHY? HOW?

GOOD MASTERS said the Trillions. Scott cursed at them.

The Trillions seemed almost to be shuffling their feet. They 'formed' uneasily. The formations would break up for no obvious reason. They would form again and write a shaky '?'. Once, they wrote 'CANOT' – 'can not'. Scott beamed at them the thought, 'You must!' But the Trillions only shuffled and shifted, making tiny meaningless blobs and shapes.

By now, Scott's mind was leaden and stupid. It was telling him, 'No more'. Stubbornly, he resisted. TELL ME ABOUT HOME PLANET, he wrote. Now he needed to write down the words if only to be able to concentrate on them.

The Trillions tumbled, twinkled, made nonsense. Scott mumbled, 'Morons! Idiots!' and kicked at a sheet of paper covered with Trillions. Then he began to undress. Washing his face, his hands seemed to be touching some-one else's skin. He looked at his watch: 2.35 in the morning.

'You've had it,' Scott said to his own reflection in the mirror.

He put on his pyjama trousers, fell into bed and turned out the light. 'You won't be able to sleep,' he told himself miserably – and, instantly, fell into the huge, deep, leaden sleep of complete exhaustion.

In the dark, the Trillions formed. They came from every corner of the room, from the fibres of the carpet, from the cracks in the floorboards. They meshed and geared, climbed and rolled, linked and interlinked. Soon there was a pile of Trillions a foot, eighteen inches, high. Still they linked and interlinked. Now they were climbing. They made a dark, dimly glittering patch on the blanket at the foot of Scott's bed. The patch became a wave that travelled towards Scott's head.

Scott groaned and turned in his bed. He lay on his back. A little flow of Trillions fell, like sand, from the sheet on to his neck. They looked like a glittering, moving stain. More Trillions followed. Scott twitched and muttered.

The Trillions formed a spearhead. It crept upward over his neck – over the lobe of his ear – into the ear: then retreated. Three more spearheads formed and probed his nostrils, his mouth, his eyelids. Then a little river crept from his neck, down over his chest and spread into a dark pool over his heart. This too retreated. Now the Trillions were almost still, as if thinking out their next move.

In the dim light from the street that filtered into the room through the curtains, they glittered darkly with each tiny movement. Scott slept on, undisturbed.

There was another wave of movement. Two streams of Trillions crept out from a pool in the hollow of Scott's neck. The streams elongated and climbed the sides of his neck, his jaw, his ears. They reached his temples. Here, the streams thickened, forming two solid pools linked by a *thin dark line. More streams stretched out like tentacles: more pools formed at the end of each stream. Now Scott was covered by a crude skeleton – a child's drawing, lines and blobs, of a human body – made of Trillions. There were pools of Trillions in the palms of his hands, on his feet, over his heart and stomach, in the pulses of his neck and wrists. The pools were linked by thin lines of Trillions and this thin line was itself linked to the main mass of Trillions on the floor beside the bed.*

Scott slept.

Scott dreamed.

But was it a dream?

He was on the planet of the Trillions. It was a raging, tearing hell.

The wind. The Wind! It screamed and roared and bellowed. It blasted and bored, tunnelled and chiselled. The great red rocks were gouged as if they were potter's clay. The wind had iron fingertips that wiped across them horizontally, tearing furrows and seams into the rocks, sculpting them into nightmare shapes. Spires and spikes swayed and tottered. When they fell, the Wind took the hard dust and fragments and used them to sharpen its claws. Even as you watched, the top of a mountain, savaged by the Wind, would surrender: its throat cut, the gigantic rocky head would be snatched up by the screaming Wind – hurtle, like a stone from a giant sling, across the reeling landscape – smash itself in a fury of fragments and a tearing cloud of dust against another mountain – while the Wind raged and roared in triumph, ready to strike again.

The Wind, Scott somehow knew, never stopped. The sky was a vicious, lurid green, filled with flying clouds. They rolled end over end, like tumbleweed, until they were torn to shreds by the wind. Or until they exploded in a sheet of flame, ignited by the clash and flash of colliding rocks. The sky was gas, the clouds were gas, and the gases were enemies. Their war, Scott knew, never ended.

Scott travelled with the Wind. If he still had a body, it was dust – for no human body could survive for a moment the hideous, never-ending gale. He travelled where it took him, sometimes at unthinkable speeds, sometimes caught in a whirlpool where he spun and spun, dizzied by the whirl of red rocks around him. Once, the Wind took him to an area of calm – a pocket between mountains where the Wind flogged itself into nothingness. Now he could study and observe. But there was nothing to see beneath him, dust – with still finer dust streaming from its surface to follow the Wind. Around him, rock. Above him, the ghastly sky with three of the planet's seven moons visible. Somehow, Scott knew there were seven.

A hundred feet above his area of calm the Wind screamed and raged. Scott saw an enormous boulder, carried by the Wind, smash the mountain peak above him. There was a crashing impact that shivered the sandy dust below him into ripples – a sheet of flame as a cloud exploded in the sky – a spattering dash of wetness from the vanished cloud – then a dreadful note began to sound, organ tones from hell. It grew and grew until even the Wind could not be heard. It grew until the rocky surfaces around him began to shudder and crumble. A few rocks fell, then more, then a landslide. Still the note swelled and grew. Soon Scott knew, the planet would be shaken to death by its vibrations.

Then he saw Trillions.

They were everywhere. They linked, formed, swarmed, crowded and surged up the walls and over the broken tops of the mountain. They filled holes, craters, gaps. As they finished their work, the unbearable note became bearable.

Now still more Trillions began to build. The top of the mountain rose again: it was made of Trillions. The wind, which had invaded the calm area, once more passed over it.

The note was gone.

Beneath him, the Trillions still poured out. Where did they come from? There! – a cleft in the rocks. Scott pointed his mind at it and entered the cleft. His body, if he had one, followed.

He was underground.

How calm!' he thought. Order and calm! Smooth walls, made of Trillions. Geometrical walls, like a maze. To baffle the Wind? He could still hear its roar. Farther on, the sound died. Silence. He went on.

Light! A dim light from the walls or within the walls. The Trillions glittered. Did they make the light, or reflect it?

A sound. A melody, almost. For the sound was many sounds, layers upon layers of sound, like music. It came from somewhere ahead of him.

The walls widened, the light grew brighter, the sound swelled – and he was *there*. In the hall of the Masters!

He was overcome, baffled by a thousand questions. How did he know this cavern was the hall of the Masters? He knew, that was enough. Where are the Masters? What could he say to them, offer them? Why want to give them something? He felt a flood of – reverence, worship? – for these unseen Masters: then a human scorn for himself. Worship! He was being stupid.

'I should have knocked,' he said out loud, cheekily.

In his mind, he heard all the Masters reply. 'There was never a door to keep you from us.' Scott seemed to hear or feel a wave of comfortable laughter. He felt himself smile and thought for a moment that he could see himself standing there, dressed in pyjama trousers and with rumpled hair. Impossible. Concentrate on the Masters. Where are they?'

'Here,' said all the voices.

But Scott could not see them. He saw glittering arches and chambers, vaults and turrets – but even as he looked at them, they seemed to shift and change. Trillions? Trillions constantly forming and reforming?

'Here,' repeated the voices.

A web, floating. Many colours. Or a moving curtain, blown by a breeze? No, a mesh – a circuit, almost. No, a field made of luminous threads—

'Difficult, very difficult,' said the voices sympathetically.

'I can't make my eyes focus properly,' said Scott.

'Close them,' replied the voices. 'Then you will see.'

He closed his eyes. Something warm touched him. Far from flinching, he reached out his hand to the welcome presence. He was led forward, then his hand was placed on something of the same warmth.

'Can't I look with my eyes?'

'Now you can.'

And he could see it quite well, though it was very bright and blurred. It was a great three-dimensional, mesh-like structure, infinitely complicated and lovely. He could not see it all. His eyes were playing tricks. It was luminous. It had Trillions in it. It was warm. It was alive.

'Is this – you?' he asked the Masters.

'Is this – you?' echoed the Masters, jokingly – and flashed at him a thousand images of himself in the space of a second – baby, eat, bigger, cut finger, home, circus, sleep, second prize, climb tree, be kind, bully, Sherlock Holmes, Trillion Truck . . .

The images ended: Scott found himself laughing. 'Difficult, very difficult,' he echoed the Masters. 'There's a lot of me. Is there,' he asked seriously, 'even more of you?'

'Close your eyes,' said the voices.

He closed them and saw. The Wind! Tearing, clawing, beating! The green sky, the tumbling clouds! Seven suns, spinning! He let his fingers rest more lightly on the mesh, the veil, the web, that was the Masters. Instantly the pictures in his mind, the sounds in his ears, grew still more clear. He was vibrating in sympathy with their nerves, their eyes, their computer, their brain.

A message! A message of danger, violence, destruction! It rippled urgently through the mesh; centred on one of many points where a thousand glistening, luminous strands interlinked. His mind saw a quick vision of a huge smash of rocks; his ear heard once more the unbearable note made by the victorious Wind; his brain felt the commands tugging the strands of the mesh, flickering through it, darting to and from the Masters' brains. He seemed to hear a command, feel the Trillions link and form in obedience, see them sent, tiny and silent, into battle against the howling Wind yelling its battle cry—

'Yes, all the time,' the Masters answered Scott's unspoken question. 'It grows stronger. Always stronger. All the time, we fight the Wind – build what it tears down – protect what it destroys . . .'

'But why, why?' demanded Scott. Part of his mind could see, under the hideous green sky, the legions of the Trillions swarming into eternal battle. Still the note sounded.

'To save our world.' The note was louder! It made the mesh throb and tremble. It shook the very walls of the Master's cavern.

'But *why?*' pleaded Scott. Trillions built, the Wind destroyed. Yet still they built and still the Masters' will sent them into battle, reformed their broken ranks, planned their assaults, patched the crumbling planet. The Wind howled and stored up vengeance: the Masters made their strange music and healed the wounds. Why?

The note faded. The Trillions had won. The mesh made its soft, gentle, vibrant music again. Peace, for a moment.

'Was there really ever a peace on this planet?' Scott thought.

'Never,' replied the Masters.

'Were there ever trees and plants, animals and . . . a proper life?'

'We understand you. No, never.'

'Was there ever happiness, something to fight for?'

'Never.'

'Then why? Why do you go on?'

There was a pause and Scott, waiting for their reply, heard only the soft music of the mesh. At last they replied.

'We must serve the Master,' said the Masters. 'The Master of everything. The Master of all planets, all lives, all of us, each single Trillion.'

'And the Trillions?'

'Through us, they serve the Master too.'

The mesh hummed gently. The Trillions that made the walls of the cavern shifted, twinkling and changing colour. Now the walls glowed purple, tinged with gold. The mesh vibrated, pleased. A veil of colour rose from it like a mist to thank them.

But the alarm tugged the mesh again, plucking it fiercely and urgently, here – there – in three places. The veil fled from the walls, wove itself in the mesh, became part of it.

The note of the Wind began to sound, louder and louder and LOUDER—

The mesh trembled, slackened, tautened again. Commands crackled from it like sparks flying up a chimney. The note was LOUDER. A wall of Trillions fell, reformed, rebuilt. The note was LOUDER. The wall fell again and struggled to rise. A hole in the mesh! Energy from it poured in burning arcs. The Masters' minds clashed and fumbled, reached out, took hold, linked, clenched – the hole closed. But the note was LOUDER.

Outside, Scott's mind saw a mountain shudder – tilt – split – explode – fly into a million bombs and arrows and hurtling masses that tore ground, burst clouds, smashed more mountains. The Wind screamed and yelled and sounded its war note. The Planet began to shake and thunder. A mountain fell into a monstrous gash that closed like jaws and crushed it to screaming, molten lava that jetted into the sky. Clouds caught fire. Flaming shreds were carried away by the Wind, thundering in the darkening sky. And the note was louder, louder, LOUDER!

Unbearable! Scott clung to the mesh with all his strength. But the lifeline was jerking, tugging, wrenching, writhing. Unbearable! He fell on his knees and let the mesh jerk and throw him anywhere. Only his hand mattered, he must not lose his grip. The mesh shuddered, slackened, tautened and bounded, flinging him across the cavern. The floor tore him. He felt the skin on his knees tearing, shredding.

'Hold on!' cried the mesh. 'Hold on!'

Cliffs shuddered and slid, skies flamed, mountains burst, continents heaved—

A hole in the mesh! Getting bigger!—

A thousand million Trillions, a mountain of them, swallowed by a jagged, smoking, dragon's mouth gaping wider and wider in the ground!—

The sound became a Thing, a pounding triphammer to beat the world to pieces!—

The mesh writhed – snapped – ripped – sundered – gave a mighty cry 'HOLD ON!' – then finally and for all time, was broken.

Scott screamed and let go.

Someone kept asking the same question, so he concentrated and tried to answer it. It was a long fight through the woolliness and greyness and back into the light. It took a long time to find the right answer and speak it, but at last he managed.

'Friend,' said Scott. Then opened his eyes.

It was Icarus bending over him. Good, thought Scott. Good old Icarus. I'm alive, then. He decided to prove he was alive by sitting up in bed. But moving his knees hurt so much that he gasped and lay back again on the pillows.

'Scott!' said Icarus. 'Well, thank God . . .' His face had an expression on it that Scott had never seen before, but was glad to see now.

'Where's mother?' Scott said.

'At the doctor's.'

'Is she ill?'

'No, you lunatic, *you're* ill. You've been ill for two days. Scott, what happened that night? How the hell did you get your knees in that state?'

'You asked me that before, didn't you?' said Scott.

'I've been asking you that – and other questions, any questions – for the last two days. What *happened* to you?'

'I don't know,' Scott muttered vaguely. He closed his eyes to give himself time to think. He came to a decision. He would tell Icarus.

'You can't get yourself into that condition and not know how—'

Scott opened his eyes, fixed them on Icarus, and said, 'I've been on the planet of the Trillions. That's where my knees got damaged. Right?'

'All right,' said Icarus, after a silence. 'Tell me the easy part first. Exactly *how* did you get your knees damaged on the Trillions' *planet*?'

'I was clutching on to the sort of mesh thing. It's all you can see of the Masters. The planet was shaking itself to pieces. The Masters were fighting to keep it in one piece. They use the Trillions just as we thought – to mend the planet itself. Ecology, remember?'

'Your knees.'

'I think I was shown the planet at the very moment when the last disaster hit it. I think I saw the beginning of the end. The Masters form this mesh, like a complicated street map or spider's web. Brain centre, everything. They radiate commands and the Trillions obey. The mesh began to shake. I was holding on to it and got flung about, on my knees. They got torn up on the floor. That's all.'

Icarus stood up, slowly. 'You've been pretty sick, Scott,' he said. 'And you still sound ill to me.'

'You don't believe me?'

'I must believe you. Your story is as good an explanation as any for the damage you've done yourself. You couldn't have done it just lying in bed – yet you were lying in bed. You haven't been out of bed for two days. So – yes, I believe you.'

'No, you don't,' said Scott. 'How can you? How can anyone?'

'Then make me believe you. Tell me the rest.'

'I will, Icarus. But you will never believe me. You can't. No one can.'

He could see that he had hurt Icarus but did not care. Why? He thought he saw the reason. 'It's all so – important, Icarus,' he went on. 'Nothing matters except the truth. Now I know the truth. I've seen it and touched it and heard it make a colossal noise in my ear. So never mind if you can't believe me. Just listen.'

He told Icarus everything. Then, next day, told his story again to Icarus, Bem, Mina and Panda. 'So you see,' he ended, 'they're friends.'

By now, his mind was completely made up. These four were to be the jury: but he, Scott, was to be the judge. They could listen to the evidence, weigh it up, make a recommendation: but only he, Scott could deliver the verdict – and carry it out.

Chapter Nine

Plan A was in operation. The world shook with explosions.

A bird fell from a tree. Panda picked it up. She looked up at Scott with her great black eyes and showed the bird to him. 'It's dead,' she whispered.

'Yes, I know. Others will die, thousands of them. But millions and millions will live. It's not the end of the world, Panda.'

'But it's *dead* . . .'

'It's not the end of the world,' he repeated, knowing that what he meant was not what she meant.

'It's the end of *its* world. The poor little thing, it's not fair, it's all wrong—'

'I know, Panda.'

'But you've got to *do* something – your Trillions—'

'I will. I promise you.'

He did.

What he did was almost a joke. It was Bem who suggested it. The four of them – Icarus, Panda, Bem and Scott – had been sitting round the living-room table. The dead bird lay in the centre of it. They had stared at it, thinking and thinking. Somehow Plan A had to be stopped. But how?

Bem suddenly got up and walked from the room. When he came back, he was carrying Scott's father's shotgun. It was a beautiful gun, one of a pair made by the most famous London gunsmith 100 years ago. There were few things Mr Houghton valued more than his shotguns.

'For heaven's *sake*!' shrilled Panda, 'if Mr Houghton finds you with that he'll *murder* you—!'

Bem put the gun down carefully on the sofa and stood in front of Panda. 'All right,' he said, 'let's pretend you are Scott's father. That's right, stand up. You've caught me with the gun. Now murder me!'

'Don't be stupid,' began Panda, weakly.

'I'm deadly serious. Do what I say. Pretend it's all happening. You've found me with the gun, you're angry, you intend to punish me. What do you do?'

'I – hit you, I suppose . . .'

'Then come on and hit me! Stand closer. Closer still. Now, pretend to hit me!'

Panda swung her arm feebly and brushed Bem's face with her hand.

'I said HIT me.'

She hit his shoulder with her fist, quite hard.

'That's better!' said Bem, looking owlish and pleased.

'I don't see much point in this,' Icarus began.

'I wish you'd put that gun *away*,' begged Panda.

'No, wait a moment. Let me go on. I did something wrong. Something to do with weapons. I *attacked* Mr Houghton, or seemed to. So now Mr Houghton can attack me. You've just seen it happen. Right?'

'Oh, all right. But I wish you'd put that *gun* away—'

'Now we are going to do it all over again,' said Bem cheerfully. He picked up the gun. 'Here I come. Priceless weapon. Panda, get ready to hit me again. Well come on! I'm all ready to be hit! What are you waiting for?'

'But I can't, not now,' said Panda.

'Why not?'

'Because you're carrying the gun!'

'Well, I won't hurt you with it, my finger's nowhere near the trigger.'

'It's not *you* I'm worrying about, stupid, it's the *gun*! Suppose I hit you and you *dropped* it . . . !'

She shuddered at the thought. Bem chuckled. 'No, you can't do much when the gun and I are together, can you?' he said. 'Well, there you are, then. I'll put it away now.' He marched out of the room, beaming.

'Wipe it down with the oil rag before you—' Scott shouted after him – then stopped and whistled. 'He's right, you know!' he said, wonderingly. 'Good old Bem! He's right!'

And he and Icarus began to chuckle, then to roar with laughter.

The plan worked at first.

Next day, when the soldiers were getting ready to obey

orders and blast more Trillions, there were serious difficulties. Overnight, the Trillions had formed into great glittering mounds. These mounds appeared only where there were weapons – the very weapons that were to be used against the Trillions.

Even to reach them, the soldiers had to sweep aside billions of Trillions. So there could be no question of using the weapons. How could you fire your TNW Mk III if the target was a mound of Trillions piled against someone else's TNW Mk III? How could a Navy corvette fire on a huge heap of Trillions with another Navy ship in the middle of it? How could aircraft drop bombs if the target area contained other fighting ships or aircraft or soldiers or guns?

For the first time in weeks, the world held its sides and laughed.

The laughter lasted until the General and his staff found the answer. 'In a word,' he said, 'mobility. Constant movement.

'Particularly aerial movement. The Trillions have only limited mobility. They can move as fast as foot soldiers, as fast as road vehicles, as fast as ships. What is more, they never grow tired, blast them. But they cannot move as fast as aircraft. So provided that we are prepared to accept substantial losses of material – of guns, motor vehicles, buildings, ammunition dumps and so forth – we can still attack the Trillions effectively.

'Now, gentlemen, are we prepared to accept such losses? Good. Then let us get to work and find out how best to *outpace* the Trillions – to march faster than them, so to speak. Then we can attack them from the air – and accept losses of our own material on the ground.

'Agreed? Good . . .'

So Bem's plan – Operation Shotgun, he had called it – began to weaken. He strengthened it by asking Scott to send Trillions to military centres – to buildings, war offices, airfields and any big, important centres that could be found. Icarus helped, Scott directed, Trillions travelled the night skies in vast armies. But as time passed, the General found answers. The roar of nuclear weapons began to be heard all over the world.

A bird fell from a tree. And once again Panda picked it up, showed it to Scott and said, 'You've got to *do* something.'

They were back where they had started.

'Plan B,' said the General.

Plan A had, after seven months, failed. Some Trillions, some experts said, had been destroyed by the nuclear blasts. Others said that if any had been destroyed – which they doubted – they were too few to matter. And the price had been too high.

But the Trillions were no longer 'forming', said the first experts. Wasn't that a victory? Too many trees were dying, said the second experts. Too much grassland was turning to mud, too many birds were falling from the trees, too many fish were floating belly-up in the oceans and rivers and lakes. Wasn't that defeat?

'Plan B,' said the General; and set his jaw more firmly. 'We have no alternative. Plan B.'

The world listened and wondered and worried itself sick. Scott judged. He judged the General and found him wanting. The General had changed and was still changing. The leathery skin seemed to be dusted over. The sharp, decisive voice began to bark. The eagle eyes began to glare and the flesh under them seemed puffy. The world was on his back and Scott judged it too heavy. 'There can be no retreat!' the General proclaimed. 'We must press home our attack and increase the pressure constantly. There is no other way.'

'Oh, isn't there?' thought Scott – but said nothing. 'Let my jury give an opinion,' he thought to himself.

'I hate it, all of it,' said Panda. 'The guns, the soldiers, the stupid new exterminators spoiling the town and the poor birds dying – I hate it and loathe it and wish I were dead!'

'I like some of the soldiers,' said Mina. 'I like Billy. But I don't like the Major. And I quite like the General. And I like Trillions.' She looked down contentedly at her latest bracelet.

'It's difficult,' said Bem. 'It's not one thing, it's lots of things, all interfering with each other . . .' Scott listened carefully. 'You remember when we were all asking Friend or Foe? Well, it was the wrong question, really. We should have been asking whether the Trillions were Guilty or Not Guilty. And we know, through Scott, that they're Not Guilty. They're innocent. They're neutrals! So it all comes back to us in the end. Us humans—'

'Bem's right,' said Icarus. 'I couldn't stand the General at first. I hated what he thought and did, what he stood for. He's a sort of walking calamity. Yet he must do what he does, it's all he knows. And now I find myself sorry for him. But even more sorry for us – all of us, everyone in the world—'

Scott studied Icarus as he spoke, and judged. The mended face, the damaged hands, the nervous mouth, the brilliant, restless, brooding, unhappy brain that lit the eyes . . . Scott judged and thought, 'No, not him. He's the other side of the General. He sees white where the General sees black and vice versa. And Icarus, with his singed wings, doesn't even want to fly any more. No, not him.'

Later, they switched on the television. Panda would not watch. She knew, she said, what it would be – Trillions, bombs, soldiers. She was right. The picture came to light and the hearty voice boomed (strange how, these days, the TV announcer's voices were always hearty and booming!) 'A new move of profound importance . . . by international agreement, a concentrated drive that promises to rid the world, finally and definitely, of the alien menace of the Trillions . . .'

Then there was the General's face. 'Plan B . . .' said the General.

'No,' said Scott. 'Not Plan B. But the world must be given something to remember. "Hate me" . . .'

He went to his room, closed the door and prepared for a hard night's work.

Two days later, his judgement was carried out; the Trillions began to form.

They formed a mighty tower that enclosed the General's headquarters. They made nightmare forts that rose from the sea and grew, minute by minute, until they soared into the sky. They built strange mazes in the middle of cities that cut the familiar streets into new patterns. They blocked runways and railroads, filled tunnels and motorways. Plan B, like most of the world's aircraft, never left the ground.

Icarus burst into Scott's room. 'What the devil are you doing?' he demanded. 'Have you gone quite mad?'

'Don't interrupt, I'm concentrating.'

'For God's sake—' began Icarus. Then the boy stared at the man and the man went away.

On the third day, Scott said to his parents and to Icarus, Bem, Panda and Mina. 'Come with me. This is the end. It's going to be worth seeing.'

'I'm making a new bracelet—' said Mina.

'I'd come if I were you. And Bem, I'd bring your camera.'

Scott led them to the end of the jetty that speared into the waters of Harbourtown West. 'We've got about three minutes before it begins,' he told them.

'But what—?'

'I'm glad you brought your cine camera, Icarus. I'd use the wide angle lens. And the tripod.'

Nobody spoke for two minutes. A motorboat sped across the harbour and its wake slapped wavelets against the piles of the jetty. There were several sail-boats out at sea.

'Will they be all right when it happens—' asked Mrs Houghton quietly.

'Oh yes. I'm not the General, mum. No bangs.'

'You're a strange son for any mother to have,' she replied.

Stranger than she knows, thought Scott. From now until

134

the end of my life. It's like holding a pair of scales, water in the pan at one end and weights at the other. And there's a hole in the water pan and someone keeps changing the weights. Yet I've got to keep the balance, always . . .

He looked at his watch. 'Now!' he said. 'It should be now! I'm telling them as hard as I can.'

They obeyed. From the jetty, you could hear a rustling sound. A fizzing. It came from everywhere – from the water, from the town, from the boards beneath their feet. Then, suddenly, the town began to shimmer. The bottoms of the houses became indistinct. The water around them fizzled and puckered.

'Away!' shouted Scott. 'Away, away!'

The houses were veiled in a glittering, shimmering mist. You could not pick out the houses any more, they were hidden—

'It's the Trillions!' screamed Panda. 'They're going up!'

Mina screamed with fright and began to cry.

'Don't, don't cry, it's quite all right!' cried Scott. He turned his face to the sky and shouted 'Away!'

Now Trillions were boiling from the water and leaping for the sky; clouding and crowding from streets and houses and cracks between paving stones, raining upwards, hissing and hurtling. The sky was still bright but the air around them was dark with Trillions. Mina was beating at her clothes, yelling in panic. Scott did not even hear her. He stood as if in a trance, murmuring 'Away, away, away!'

The town was shut off from them now. And in every other town and city in the world, it was the same – the whispering hordes of Trillions, mounting to the skies, clambering over each other to escape when trapped, glinting and turning and linking, then soaring up and up in spiralling corkscrews, constantly building up their acceleration from each other.

Scott was his former self again – a schoolboy with a camera. 'Look! Over there! You can see the church, the base of the Trillions cloud is lifting! The colours! Icarus, I'm giving it 150th at f.11, is that right on your meter? Look at the spire, the spire!'

It was incredible. The Trillions now formed a massive pall over the town – not a cloudy or smoke-like mass, but a glittering, colour-changing, living thing—

'Look up! Look up!' shouted Bem.

Above them, the pall swirled slowly in a huge circle. As they watched, a vast hole formed. The swirling became swifter and a hissing noise filled the air. Then light flooded through the centre of the vortex – the blue of the sky! The hissing became louder, louder – the waves in the harbour ruffled – countless hordes of Trillions were swept into the throat of the vortex and, hissing, were flung upwards and onwards, into the blue.

'They spin each other, that's it!—' Icarus was shouting. 'That must be it, each one gives the other a nudge and then you get this colossal acceleration in the vortex—'

His voice was drowned by a screeching hiss. Tops of little waves broke off and jumped into the air. Panda was holding her skirt down with both hands and laughing. Mrs Houghton cried,

'The yachts! – those boys in the yachts!'

Then all at once it was over. The sky was dark where

the Trillions blotted out the sunshine. The air was still. Harbourtown West, tranquil in the grey light, was itself. Boats bobbed in the harbour and out at sea, the yachts heeled when they caught a breeze. Slowly, it became lighter and lighter. At last the sun shone through and the sky was azure blue, dotted with white clouds.

'Gone!' said Mina. 'They've all gone!' She held up her brown wrist. It was encircled with a strip of glue-y card-board. Not a Trillion remained.

'All gone!' said Mina.

She was not quite right. Here and there, people still found Trillions. They had been trapped underneath heavy objects, locked in cracks and crevices. People kept them as souvenirs. Mina found enough to make a new bracelet in time.

Plan B was never put into force. The lorries rumbled away. Billy and the Major went with them. When you switched on the television, you no longer saw the General's face. The Exterminator was itself exterminated and Scott returned his Trillion Truck. He and the rest of the gang shouted, 'Hi ho Trillions!' for the last time.

Icarus stayed on at the Houghtons for two weeks of messing about in boats, then he too had to go. He put out his hand to shake Scott's and said, 'I suppose it's all up to you now.' They stood there rather stupidly, hand clasping hand, trying to think of something to say. Eventually, Icarus said, 'There's trouble blowing up in the Far East . . .'

'I know. I've been following it in the papers, on television—'

'There'll always be trouble somewhere, I suppose,' said Icarus. 'Hate. Fighting. Things getting out of balance.'

'Yes.'

'Well, do the best you can, Scott. I mean, you can't do everything, but—'

'I've got friends,' smiled Scott, cocking an eye at the sky. 'I can always call them when I need them.'